QUITE POSSIBLY FINAL

FREEMAN UNIVERSE

PATRICK O'SULLIVAN

dunkerron press

A Dunkerron Press™ Book.

Copyright © 2022 by Patrick O'Sullivan

PatrickOSullivan.com

Illustration © Tom Edwards

TomEdwardsDesign.com

ISBN-13: 978-1-62560-029-5

ISBN-10: 1-62560-029-1

BOOKS IN THIS SERIES

Novels:

Quite Possibly Alien

Quite Possibly Allies

Quite Possibly Heroes

Quite Possibly Final

Novellas, Novelettes, and Short Stories:

Quite Possibly True

Quite Possibly False

1

C iarán mac Diarmuid shoved his way through the pre-
holiday crush as shopkeepers and their suppliers
raced to stock temporary shelves with whatever yet
remained salable on the planet.

The harvest festival on Prescott Grange began on the
morrow, and despite the recent chaos in the skies above the tiny
town of First Landing, there would be a festival, and it would be
festive, else there would be hell to pay. He'd heard that senti-
ment expressed in a dozen different forms from a dozen pairs of
lips as he pressed forward beneath the spreading canopies of a
dozen marquees, the wind flapping the fabric overhead as
tradesmen scurried and cooks cooked. The jostling heat of
flesh on flesh, the mingling scents wafting from ten score ovens
and hobs created a moist and fragrant microclimate, dripping
condensation from transparent view sheets meant to keep the
wind at bay. The sun sat low enough this late in the day, and in
the local year, that it slashed beneath the great canopies,
casting long shadows across the chaos of kiosks and cart-stalls
gathered from around the planet.

Tomorrow would be a madhouse, as nearly every surviving

adult and child descended upon First Landing to celebrate the
bringing in of the crops, as they did every year, and the survival
of the community, as they never had before. On any other day
Ciarán would have inhaled the energy and laughed at the
jostling, and the jokes about his height, but he was on a
mission, one he'd rather not have started, but having started,
preferred to finish as quickly and as efficiently as possible.

He'd spied the personal electronics vendor's signage from
across the marquee, and five minutes later still waded through
the crowd. When he finally arrived at the tiny kiosk he found
the shelving largely bare and the kiosk lorded over by a largely
humanoid walrus.

"I'm hunting the proprietor," Ciarán said, in Trade
Common. The walrus, of course, wasn't a walrus, but a man or
woman inside a walrus-shaped projection. This sort of fancy
dress appeared ubiquitous throughout the League, and
throughout the Federation as well. The basic outfits were fairly
inexpensive and immensely popular with children, and also
with adults on those occasions where anonymity was desired
and juvenile behavior expected.

The walrus pressed a button on its belt and the walrus
glamour disappeared.

"I am the proprietor," the shopkeeper said. He looked very
much like a walrus, both in shape and in bearing. His mustache
wiggling as his eyes sparkled with mirth.

Ciarán chuckled. "I'm—"

"The best disguises hew close to the truth," the shopkeeper
said. "Take your own, for instance."

"I'm not wearing a disguise." Ciarán stood dressed in pale
cream Consolidated Tractor Service utilities, well-used ones,
with a spot or two of grease yet on them. If he hadn't become a
merchant apprentice, he might possibly have ended up as a
tractor mechanic. And there was no rule that said a man

couldn't purchase second-hand utilities at a trade cart and wear them. Anyone might, and thus he might.

"Is that your name on the chest there?" The shopkeeper winked. "Charles."

The name patch on the utilities had made Ciarán's mind up. Of the three pairs he'd found that would fit, only this pair came with that extra benefit. "That's what it says on my work permit."

"We'll pretend it is, then. What can I help you with?"

"A handheld."

"New or second hand?"

"Second hand, unless new is cheaper."

"Depends on the plan selected."

"No plan. Pay as you go, unless prepaid is cheaper."

"I'm detecting a theme here."

Ciarán smiled. "They're running me off. Me and all the non-resident aliens. I need something so I can be reached. Something that will work on Sizemore."

"You're on the last boat out, then."

"So I hear. If I can afford it."

"It's a mandate. Even if you can't pay, they'll find a spot for you."

"It's not charity I want."

"It's not working off the debt, you mean. Working it off on Sizemore."

"Or wherever they choose to send me, afterwards."

"It's lucky you're here on setting up day, and not tonight, or tomorrow."

"It's not luck. It's a plan. I figure with the embargo starting…"

"I'll be out of stock by midnight, and don't I know it."

"We both know it. I'm not asking for a favor, but for a fair price, both of us knowing the other knows the facts, as it were."

"So we do. Do you fancy a haggle?"

"I've yet to purchase the outbound ticket. I'm not sure how much it will be."

The walrus-man smiled. "So it's a handheld and an outbound ticket to Sizemore for you?"

"And a prepaid plan, or enough money left over to pay as I go."

"We're talking about a bundle, then."

"We might be," Ciarán said. "Maybe I should go and buy the ticket, and then come back later, when I know how much I have left to spend."

"Maybe I should buy the ticket, with my local's discount, and bundle it in. You'll get more for your money that way."

"Can you do that?"

"My brother runs the ticket booth."

"My identification. It's not..."

"It's a one-way ticket, isn't it?"

"It is."

"I don't see any problem, then."

Ciarán nodded. "I guess it's a bundle I want."

"Then it is a bundle ye shall have, Charles," the Walrus man said.

"That's grand. I'd like to see the ticket, with my name on it, before we haggle."

The walrus man laughed. "Fair play to you, Mr..."

"Newton. Charles Newton."

"Wait here," the walrus-man said. He walked away a step or two, turned his back, and used his own handheld. He swiveled around to eyeball Ciarán, as he nodded and spoke into the device. After a short while he rang off and returned to his booth. "Ticket arranged. Let the haggling resume."

Ciarán chuckled. "Was I that obvious?"

"Like one beetle knows another," he said. "This walrus knows a bright tiger when he spies one."

"I—"

"We are not at war, lad, not yours and mine. We both keep the shelves stocked, the prices low, and the customer happy, each in our own way. Now do you want to match wits or not?"

"I—"

"Fair warning. If there's a penny in your pocket when we're done you're buying the drinks."

"And if there's not a penny?"

The walrus-man smiled. "There won't be."

2

The Prescott Grange locals were a fun-loving bunch and they'd been through a lot. When they blew off steam you could see the plume from orbit. That's what he'd been told, and now that he'd seen them in action, he believed it.

On Prescott Grange they didn't dress up in traditional garb, like at home, but wore the same sort of field-generators people used for fancy dress parties on Trinity Station, ones where the field surrounded the wearer and a projector painted the costume on the inside of the field.

On Trinity Station the fashion was to masquerade as the dead or as spirits, usually of famous historical figures, or characters from popular stories. Here the party theme proved animal-related, with people done up as humanoid birds, deer, foxes, martens, and whatever else the wearer fancied, including fish. He hadn't seen any whales, but he'd met a few sharks. By the time he boarded the shuttle he'd been groped by a gorilla, punched by a kangaroo, and kissed by a pig. It would have been fun at any other time, but he was on a mission, and fun was not on the agenda.

Ciarán didn't want to go to Sizemore. He *needed* to go to Unity Station, in Freeman space, for the in-person examination by the Merchant Guild's nominating committee, a make-or-break interview that would determine his future. He'd aced the merchant exam. He'd completed a successful if unconventional apprentice cruise. He'd been nominated by a nic Cartaí merchant captain.

None of that mattered, except as table stakes. The Merchant Guild's managing partners wanted to look him in the eye. To size him up in person. To judge what he was made of with their own senses. They could still blackball him, but they'd do it to his face.

He wasn't the right stuff, not according to the Guild's space-born standards, but he'd made it this far. His hands wore calluses earned from shovel and plow, there was no denying that. But he 'd clawed his way out of a gravity well, and found a ship, and found a crew. A ship and crew where he fit in. Merchant Captain Aoife nic Cartaí had made it clear. He could keep all that he'd won, but only if he followed the forms. Merchant apprentices became merchants. That, or they flamed out and plummeted back from whence they came. Soar or sink, no hovering allowed.

Given the events of his apprentice cruise and the current reputation of his ship and captain there could be no delay. A merchant's license was a one-way gate, one that led to a future amongst the stars. He needed to step through that gate now, before it slammed shut in his face.

Time was of the essence. News travelled fast. Both he and Aoife needed to outrace the myths and stories so that they might reveal the truth before falsehood became fact. The merchant captain could not be in two places at once. Fortunately, she didn't need to be. She had a merchant apprentice for just such occasions.

Quite Possibly Alien headed for Trinity Station on an urgent mission, one that didn't require the ship's merchant apprentice. A temporary situation, one that would be rectified as soon as possible, *word of a merchant*. So said his merchant captain, and so it would be. He'd said his farewells to ship and crew, and that was that. Leaving Wisp behind proved the hardest part, for him at least. The ship's cat seemed unconcerned. Carlsbad was back on board, and with the ship's cargo master, a fresh supply of augustinite, catnip by another name.

Ciarán glanced at the transport ticket in his hand. He was Charles Newton, at least for a little while. He hoped Mr. Newton was the lucky and clever sort who wouldn't be cheated into believing he'd been handed a ticket for passage and not simply a scrap of paper made to look like one. Or, if it truly proved to be a scrap of paper, he hoped that the data file on his ancient but serviceable handheld was the real deal. He'd used the information on the paper to create an electronic copy that Carlsbad said would work, even if the paper ticket wouldn't.

One way or another he was bound for Unity Station and his merchant examination. *Count on it.*

3

C iarán hitched his bug-out bag higher onto his shoulders and stepped through the troop transport's ingress hatch. His gaze followed the yellow stripe of the novice trail as it led deeper into the guts of the League military vessel. He could turn on his heel, and shove his way out the way he'd come, right up until the moment they dogged the hatch.

And then what? There was only one way out of this mess.

He took a deep breath, squared his shoulders, and marched forward.

The troop transport lay in orbit around Prescott Grange system's primary planet, a planet that until recently had hosted a massive space station, fleet refitting docks, and a pair of redundant superluminal nodes. Now the planet lay pockmarked with impact craters, orbital space lay blanketed in a thick layer of space junk, and interplanetary space hosted an ever-spreading debris field, one that would eventually clear as it succumbed to the gravity of Prescott Grange's star.

Prescott Grange wasn't a ruined system, but it was one in need of a massive cleanup effort, an effort that had already begun. Until then all non-essential personnel in the system were being evacuated to Sizemore, whether they wanted to go to Sizemore or not. Thus, the almost-empty troop transport, the last of many, and one with open seating for citizens and registered aliens stranded in the system and in need of transport. To Sizemore.

Every surface inside the troop transport had been painted a light gray. Those surfaces that met did so at right angles. Occasionally, there were black and yellow hashed warning stripes affixed to low overhead pipes and ducting, the only splashes of color other than the novice trail.

On Freeman family ships the decks and bulkheads were a patchwork of colors, painted piecemeal over the years with whatever was cheapest at the time, only ducts and conduits color-coded by function. The Merchant Guild had established a standard recommendation for coding though it wasn't yet in widespread use, and according to his instructors at the Academy, wasn't to be trusted.

Here there was nothing to trust or distrust. Cold. Uniform. Impersonal. The soul of the modern League in concrete form.

He'd grown accustomed to his own ship, *Quite Possibly Alien*, a League vessel from a different time. Dark. Sinister. Indirect. No measurable angles, just flat black curve meeting flat black curve, the hatches and airlocks sized for giants. Sized for giants and *alive*.

The novice trail directed him to the last of ten troop drop modules, one reserved for commercial passengers, mostly civilians and foreigners, not that there were many of those remaining in the system. He had expected to have the compartment to himself.

He ran his fingers along a gray bulkhead before ducking through the drop module hatch. Nothing could be felt, no yielding, no pushback, no recognition that he existed at all. He strode through the belly of a soulless machine, one that had not been quickened, nor would it ever be. He didn't know its name and it didn't matter. Some sort of number designation, LRN-TR-something. Three digits? Four?

Three digits, he decided, based on the apparent age of the crash webbing and collapsible jump seats arranged along the inner hull, a long corridor stretching fore and aft along the spine of the compartment between the uncomfortable-looking seats. The corridor could accommodate two score fast pallets parked side by side in pairs along the length of it. There were only two of the cargo movers aboard at present, each in *stay put* mode and lashed down with crash webbing just in case.

In case of what? In case of *something* that happened on League vessels that didn't happen on Freeman vessels. He'd not ever seen a lashed-down fast pallet and didn't understand the point. There weren't even webbing attachment points on Freeman fast pallets. He tried to imagine what sort of force it would take to overcome the *stay-put* field and couldn't think of anything that could dislodge a locked-down fast pallet short of a missile strike.

Duh. This superluminal might superficially resemble a merchant vessel, but a troop transport was a ship of war, in a war zone, and rigged for war. There *was* a war on, more than one, and it hadn't occurred to him that he might end up as collateral damage in a fight that had nothing to do with him.

He slowed, and glanced behind, toward the hatch, before pulling his gaze away. He didn't want to *die* on the way to Sizemore any more than he wanted to *go* to Sizemore. But he was *going* to Sizemore. He'd made his mind up and said his good-byes and there was no turning back. Sizemore, to Prix Canada, to Unity Station. The long way around, but the fast way.

And definitely not the safe way. The ten drop modules on a League troop transport were little more than active cargo pods, ones designed for delivering armored soldiers and their weapons to a planet from orbit. They were bigger and sturdier than FFEs, the self-powered shipping containers Freeman merchants used. But inside one? It felt the same. He wasn't crew. He wasn't a passenger. He was cargo. He'd eat strapped into crash webbing. He'd sleep strapped into crash webbing. Everything he did, he'd do it strapped into crash webbing.

Well, almost everything.

A portable head stood strapped near the aft bulkhead, a civilian accommodation as an afterthought. A fifty-hour superluminal transit, they'd deposit him on Sizemore Station with the crash webbing impressions still etched into his flesh.

There were plenty of empty seats in the drop module. A solitary passenger sat in a crash seat halfway down the starboard bulkhead, a well-turned-out and prosperous-looking woman in civilian dress. A grain merchant, perhaps, or someone engaged in the automated farming equipment trade. That the station hadn't fallen but broken up in orbit had saved the surface businesses from total ruin. A great deal of the planet's infrastructure had been damaged however, equipment that needed replacement, and all the commodity forecasts were in flux, the sort of flux that favored the merchant with boots on the ground.

There remained another possibility. He looked the woman over. In addition to being a breadbasket world and Forward Fleet Headquarters, Prescott Grange had been a nursery for synthetic intelligences, fifteen of them, all young, all recently evacuated on sentient ships, each a major undertaking. He expected that to be a military operation, and it looked like it from a distance, as *Quite Possibly Alien* hung in orbit and waited for commercial access to the temporary superluminal node the League had set up.

Still, restoring the system infrastructure required a civilian component. The seated woman had the bearing of a senior executive. And the wardrobe. Her *shoes* looked like they cost more than a merchant apprentice grossed in a year. He didn't know what to call her outerwear. A merchant captain's great-coat, it was *not*. *Cape* was the word that sprang to mind, the sort of anti-ballistic drape that villains sneered from behind and soaring heroes wore in animated children's dramas.

Whatever that hooded garment was called, it looked bespoke and expensive, a sort of shimmering rainbow of shifting shades that changed from copper to verdigris as he moved along the corridor relative to her. It took Ciarán a moment to realize that the cape's changing colors were mirrored by her shoes. The effect was striking, if a little over the top for a grain merchant. She had a duffel perched on the seat beside her, one that looked recently purchased and exorbitantly priced.

She *might* be involved with the synthetic intelligence evacuation. If so, she'd be a valuable contact. Even if she wasn't, it was a long journey to Sizemore, and he might learn something useful, maybe just the price of corn futures or the number of hectares a combine harvester could process in an hour, but it would be something new. Something to distract him from his own business. From his own *promises*.

Plus, he liked the challenge. He'd have to get her talking without talking himself. He might look like a Leagueman, in his Consolidated Tractor Service utilities, and he might yet pass if she wished to converse in Trade, but these people didn't, not amongst themselves. The minute he mouthed more than a word or two of erlspout the masquerade would end, and no telling what would happen then, except that he wouldn't like it.

He parked his bug-out kit two seats aft and across from her, and lowered himself into one seat further aft of his kit. She glanced at him briefly and dismissed him with a curt nod, icy and attractive, and a suitable match for someone his father's age. He tried to imagine what she would sound like when she spoke.

Put the tiara on the nightstand. That will be all, Bridget.

She glanced at him again.

He smiled.

She did not.

The compartment had an antiseptic smell, like it had been recently hosed out with industrial cleaner. There wasn't a spot of grime or a shadow, other than hers, his, and that of the two large shipping crates on the fast pallets, on the deck. Featureless air, featureless light, an environment as devoid of character as one could possibly make it. No rumble of unbalanced air handlers. No hiss of atmosphere from dust-clotted ductwork. He glanced at the crates. They were gray, like the bulkheads, with recessed latches sealed with customs tape, and unlabeled on the sides he could see from his seat. He considered getting up to inspect them more closely, but the imminent departure announcement sounded, in erlspout only, a five-minute warning, the first of three warnings.

He belted in without waiting for the two-minute warning. The buckles snapped together with a crisp click, and he pulled the webbing tight—a six-way harness he could unsnap with a single quarter-turn release, the sort of innovation that resulted from centuries of continuous improvement. He used his handheld to capture a brief recording of the device's operation. As he pocketed the multi-purpose tool he glanced up to find the woman watching. She glanced away the instant their gazes met.

He considered the harness latch. The device was likely commonplace but he hadn't seen one similar. Thinking about the trade possibilities kept his mind occupied. He didn't have to worry about what would happen in the next three minutes. The two-minute warning would sound, then the one minute, then the ingress hatch would swing closed and dog, and he would be on one side of that hatch, and everyone and everything he knew and loved would be on the other.

When the hatch opened on Sizemore it would open under the light of a foreign star. His age and the age of his friends would have diverged to some degree he couldn't calculate. A week, maybe? Certainly less than a month. If his luck held, he would make his connection to Prix Canada, and, from there, a one-way direct transit to Unity Station in the Federation, administrative center and seat of the Merchant Guild. A day or two standard and he'd be called before the Licensing Board and formally apprised of his test scores, which he knew already, and questioned about his apprentice cruise, which could go very wrong if not handled correctly.

There were three outcomes he might reasonably expect. He might be elevated to merchant. He might be forced to remain a merchant apprentice. And he might be stripped of his merchant license, prosecuted for murder, or barring that, manslaughter, and held pending trial.

Whatever the outcome, he would face the Board alone. Aoife nic Cartaí and *Quite Possibly Alien* had been ordered to Trinity Station to address the present ban on trade with the League. That he booked passage on a League vessel was technically a violation of the ban, but one he was willing to risk. He wasn't wearing the pendant spire and he might easily pass as a Leagueman otherwise, until he opened his mouth and the accent of Oileán Chléire burst from his lips.

He began tearing his unused luggage tag into pieces and balling the shreds, adhesive side out. A nervous habit, it gave his hands something to do. Once he had a pile of the little pea-sized balls he chose a target. The furthest-aft latch on one of the shipping crates. He positioned the ball, and snapped his fingers, sending the sticky ball rocketing. The adhesive ball struck the shipping container a centimeter below the hatch and stuck.

He absently flicked a half-dozen more of the tiny projectiles, each one missing the target, each one sticking to the shipping container, a ring around the lock, uniformly circular and uniformly a miss.

He glanced up as he reloaded to find the grain merchant watching.

"You're making a mess," she said.

"Yes," he said.

"Stop it."

He felt his face heat. "Yes." He pocketed the remainder of the pea-sized projectiles.

The two-minute warning sounded, and immediately afterwards, the sounds of laughter, and of voices. He couldn't see the speakers but the grain merchant could. She groaned, and muttered, "Spare me," in crisp erlspout, and then he could see them, all seven of them, four silver-antlered stags, two amber-antlered roebucks, and at their center, a golden hind, each enormously tall, so tall that their antlers seemed to scrape the deckhead. A bottle tumbled from a roebuck's pocket and they all laughed as he scrambled for it.

The one-minute warning sounded.

The grain merchant trapped the bottle beneath her heel.

"Belt in," she said. "Right now."

And the herd of drunkards did.

She kicked the bottle into her hand and tucked it beneath her duffle.

Ciarán scanned from expressionless face to expressionless face.

Okay. So she's not an ordinary grain merchant. And they're not ordinary drunks.

This had a bad feel about it. He needed to be elsewhere.

Ciarán gripped his bug-out bag's straps.

He glanced at the crash strap buckle holding him tight. His fingers hovered as he glanced at the compartment hatch.

The one-minute claxon hammered on.

The deck began to vibrate as the in-system drive spooled up.

The hatch closed.

The hatch sealed.

The claxon abruptly cut off.

Someone cursed.

Every eyeball in the compartment swiveled toward him.

That's grand. At least he'd cursed in Trade Common.

The in-system drive engaged.

4

T he troop transport accelerated abruptly, as if it were moving away from a station. He wondered if that sudden motion was necessary to the operation of the vessel, or the result of pilot's muscle memory, or an expression of League piloting doctrine. In any case it seemed consistent. Hess and Konstantine, both League pilots, handled a vessel in precisely the same way, with a sharp punch that would have spiked the inertial dampers and tossed the crockery around on a Freeman family ship. Here there wasn't any drama worth mentioning. The crash webbing dug into him hard for a ten count before the pressure let up. By then anything not strapped down would have been pasted to the stern bulkhead.

Nothing struck him or whizzed by him. Everything appeared strapped down because there wasn't anything to strap down. Only he and the grain merchant had carry-on luggage, and they'd secured it.

That lack of luggage was decidedly odder than the deer herd's holiday costumes. No one sane took a fifty-hour superluminal flight without a carry-on.

The impression of acceleration abated as the rumble of the

in-system drive settled into a steady low frequency drone. They were moving out briskly but at a constant clip. They'd continue to do so until they passed the system tripwire and the pilot kicked the superluminal drive active. Until then it would be possible to unbelt, provided there was no need for evasive action.

According to Mrs. Amati, *Quite Possibly Alien*'s weapons master, there were two types of spacers who unbelted in a war zone. Idiots and corpses. The only reason for Ciarán to unbelt was to patch a hull breach after all the idiots and corpses had been sucked clear. And only then after the fast patch dispensers were depleted or shot away. And only then after any surviving crewmen were unable to patch the breach manually.

Which meant never unbelt on a League warship.

Almost never, Amati had said. *If there's blood on the deck use your judgement.*

There wasn't blood on the deck. Not yet, anyway.

The rest of the passengers in the compartment had lost interest in him. They were now eyeballing each other.

The woman, first off. He'd been around enough starship captains to know one when he heard one. She was once either the League equivalent of a ship's captain or a former military officer. She hadn't raised her voice but her words had carried over the claxon's roar. Not just confident words but commands with muscle behind them. She was used to being obeyed, or else. Her will had the power of a natural law. *Believe it*, that tone said, and brooked no argument. He'd believed it, like any spacer with a sense of self-preservation would have.

The herd of harts and hind, now. They'd believed it too, but the command spell was beginning to wear off. The golden hind in particular had a revolutionary tilt to her crown. There was no telling if that projection hid a woman or not. He'd put money on it, though. It was the rare reveler that gender-switched their costume, and a rare man that jetted about with six women in tow. They were what they appeared, hardware-wise. And while he'd never seen a doe at the head of a herd of bucks at home, he'd seen nothing but since he'd climbed out of Trinity Surface's gravity well. The observed numbers felt truthful because they fit the prevailing order.

Everything else about that lot seemed a lie. Hard-partiers didn't follow orders and they certainly didn't do so in any coordinated way. He'd expected a scuffle over the bottle. Maybe there would still be a dust-up, but a delayed one. The lot of them together had the posture of a lit fuse. They'd expected to have the compartment to themselves, and the golden hind had expected to rule the deck. But not a minute after she'd stepped through the hatch she'd been cowed by a shiny-caped grain merchant. *The neck on that bint*, she was thinking, or would have been, if she were Freeman.

But she wasn't Freeman, nor were the others with her. He was only thinking of them as Freeman because of their costumes. And now that he thought about it, even their costumes were a lie.

He'd never seen a field projection costume until he'd arrived on Trinity Station. There they were all the rage. Seamus and Macer each owned one, with Macer's being the best that money could buy, and Seamus's being the sort of thing you couldn't buy, but an evil genius could cobble together in software.

The headdress of the costume was pretty straightforward, a collar that established a gossamer field around the wearer's head and a holo tank projector that displayed whatever the wearer wanted on the inner surface of the field. You could quite easily look like a man with a stag's head and antlers. The high-end units had cameras that tracked the wearer's facial expressions and processors that modulated the projector, so you could smile, or frown, or blink, and when you talked the lips would sync, though it might sound like you were speaking from your navel. Seamus in particular favored costumes that made him seem taller.

You could appear taller still with a second projector and field, worn as a belt, that would do the same thing as the first, only for the rest of you, and in addition, sync with the collar-projector to offset the head upwards. You couldn't make yourself appear any shorter than you were without walking around in a crouch all night, which Macer did once, with his rig set up to look like a scowling Seamus. You could, however, prance around per normal and appear toweringly tall, which was something mummers did at birthday parties and holiday parades on the Arcade. Just as the collar tracked your facial expressions, the belt projector tracked your legs and torso so that it seemed you were a walking giant, although often one that took mincing steps.

There were two things you couldn't do in the getup and maintain the illusion. You couldn't sit down. Not without it looking like your giant legs had sunk through the deck. And you couldn't scramble around on the deck for a bottle. Not without it looking like you'd sunk in nearly to your waist.

Neither of which had happened with this lot.

So this herd of fake revelers had better tech than he'd ever seen. Or they were wearing headdresses only, and were all naturally, enormously, tall.

The alert claxon blurted three times.

Tripwire.

The in-system drive kicked off and the world went ballistic for an instant.

He glanced at the grain merchant.

She sat watching him.

"Exhale," she said. She tugged her crash harness tight, demonstrating.

"Sure," he muttered, and reached for his own harness.

The Templeman drive engaged.

5

The nausea felt like it would never end. This wasn't like the sudden on and off sickness when *Quite Possibly Alien*'s superluminal drive engaged. The gut twisting began instantly and didn't let up. He pulled the get-sick bag free from its fixture and held it at arm's length. He was a long-haul spacer. He was supposed to be hardened to jump sickness. He'd taken a pair of training jumps and a single transit aboard *Impossible Bargains* but this was his first Templeman translation aboard a League warship. Clearly his stomach didn't like being yanked into a bubble universe any more than the rest of him.

He took deep breaths.

That didn't help.

He swallowed, and gritted his teeth, and took more deep breaths.

It felt like he was getting his guts under control when one of the roebucks spewed, and spattered the deck just as Ciarán inhaled.

"You'll clean that," the grain merchant said, meaning the

roebuck would, but by the time Ciarán had figured out she wasn't speaking to him, he'd thought about it, *cleaning that*, and the smell was in him, and it was like a raging tide erupting inside him, and no reef strong enough to fight it. He might have missed the sick bag himself if he hadn't had it in his hand, bending over and retching at the same time.

When he was done spewing, he cinched the sack of mess tight and fished in his bug-out bag for a water bottle. His guts still churned but there wasn't much left in him for them to work with.

A rinse packet landed in his lap.

He glanced up to find the woman watching.

"It happens to the best of us," she said.

"Yes," he replied, one of three erlspout words that Carlsbad, *Quite Possibly Alien*'s League-born cargo master, had cleared for usage. The other two words were "no" and "sure." "Yes" and "no" because they weren't words he'd ever used, and "sure" because it sounded exactly like what the Ellis called the farrier back on Oileán Chléire. Don't utter another word, Carlsbad had said. *Else you'll be unmasked. And detained.*

He couldn't afford to be detained. He was cutting it fine as it was.

Maybe if the compartment hadn't been so clean and fresh to begin with, the stink and mess from the retching wouldn't have been so eye wateringly vile. But it was. And stomach roiling. So when the roebuck unbelted, at first Ciarán was thankful there was at least one idiot amongst them to clean up the mess, but then the other roebuck unbelted as well, and they both stepped over the mess, and shoved past him and the grain merchant, and he thought well, they're going to the lashed-down head for some cleaning supplies, but they weren't, they were going to the lashed-down crates, and both of them began tearing off the customs tape, and one of the stags tossed them a folding knife, and one of the roebucks caught it, and slashed the tie downs free, then they had the latches open, and they tossed the case lid aside, and bent to reach inside.

Ciarán glanced at the grain merchant, and she had gone all stiff and still, her face a placid mask, only her eyes alive, as they glanced from the roebucks to the rest of the herd that hadn't moved but seemed to be waiting for something. He had a pretty good idea what they were waiting for, because it was all beginning to slot into place now, and the only thought that kept running through his brain like a mantra was that he didn't want to be detained, detained, detained, which he might be, if he unbelted and stopped them, or tried, but there wasn't blood on the deck, not yet, anyway, and what use was good advice if you ignored it.

The first roebuck pulled a pulse rifle from the case, an Oscar-Mike-nineteen, and tossed it to one of the stags. The second did the same. They were both Mark One stroke six models, cheap and ubiquitous because the stroke sixes tended to overheat and jam. Gene-keyed, he couldn't have fired one even if he'd been able to reach out and snag it as it passed. Only a Huangxu or Huangxu Eng could use that weapon. The only reason he had even recognized the model was because the Iron Fists of Empire, a mercenary company he'd accidentally become responsible for, kept overheating and jamming the blasted things during live-fire exercises. He was expected to do something about that, but given the nature of his other responsibilities, he'd back-burnered that task.

According to Old, acting commander of the Legion of Heroes, the problem was simple and economical to fix. *Confiscate the Iron Fist's ammunition. The OM-19 remains quite effective as a club.*

The roebucks tossed a second pair of pulse rifles to the other stags. A pair of razor guns, Delta-kilo-forty-fours followed, another rubbish weapon according to Old. The tallest stag and the golden hind tucked the sidearms beneath their belts.

The quality of the weapons confirmed his suspicion. These weren't Imperial troops. They were mercenaries, or pirates, and quite possibly coin-operated ones. If he could discover the right coin they might just leave him alone, and he might yet make his connection to Prix Canada. There was no need to panic yet. He was being slowed. He wasn't being *detained*.

Ciarán began to ease his fingers toward the crash harness latch. He didn't think they were here to murder him, but they might do so if he became a problem. Being strapped down seemed tactically compromising. He glanced at the grain merchant.

She shook her head swiftly.

No.

She made a production of keeping her hands clear of the harness latch.

He followed her lead, keeping his hands clear, but nearly changed his mind when he saw what the roebucks dragged next from the shipping crate.

Bang sticks.

One for each member of the herd.

The Huangxu Eng were slave makers, ones that maintained order through terror when necessary. The bang stick was their most recent development in terror weapons. A strike from a bang stick didn't kill its victim. It simply robbed them of intellect, slowly, inevitably, in a painfully apparent manner to the victim and the victim's family alike. Multiple strikes increase the rate and severity of the damage. William Gagenot, *Quite Possibly Alien*'s victualer, had been struck six times by a Huangxu bang stick. Ciarán didn't have to imagine what such a weapon did to a man. A bang stick didn't end lives. It *destroyed* them, leaving a shoal of wounded and their caregivers in its wake. A nerve disrupter to the temple. Drawing and quartering. Crucifixion. They each seemed more humane than a bang stick strike. He glanced at the grain merchant.

Her face had grown ashen. She had recognized the weapon as well.

The golden hind unbelted and strode toward the hatch. A pair of stags unbelted and followed her. The remaining pair unbelted and stood as the golden hind worked the compartment controls. If those controls were like an FFE's controls she would be able to adjust the lighting, the temperature, the humidity, and other environmental factors. What she would not be able to do from inside the drop module was—

The compartment hatch opened.

That.

The golden hind sang out orders in Huangxu Eng. "Secure the prisoners. Ready the cargo. Do not harm the prisoners unless they fight you."

The taller of the roebucks spoke. "They will fight us."

"Maybe," the golden hind said.

"Certainly they will fight," the largest of the stags rumbled. "After the cargo is readied."

"Yes, Great Lord," the second roebuck said.

Which confirmed what Ciarán thought he'd heard. The big stag and the roebucks, at least, had no intention of letting them go. The grain merchant and he would fight because they'd be given no choice.

The bulk of the herd headed through the hatch.

The hatch remained open.

One of the roebucks gripped Ciarán's bug-out bag. He pointed the pulse rifle at Ciarán one-handed until Ciarán let go of the backpack's straps.

The second roebuck took the grain merchant's duffel and

piled it into a seat beside Ciarán's bag, in sight but out of reach. The bottle the grain merchant had tucked beneath the bag seemed to have disappeared.

One roebuck kept its weapon trained on them while the other disassembled the weapons crate, tossing the flat panels sternward in a jumbled heap. He slashed the customs tape on the remaining crate with a folding knife and worked the latches, tossing those panels aside as well until the contents were revealed.

An autodoc, one lying on its back atop the bottom of the crate and the locked-down fast-pallet. The autodoc was active, with someone in it.

The roebuck disengaged the stay-put field and shouted in Huangxu Eng. "Move your legs!"

Ciarán pretended not to understand. He couldn't tell if the grain merchant pretended ignorance or not, but neither of them moved their legs.

The roebuck rammed the fast pallet forward. Ciarán lifted his legs as did the grain merchant.

The autodoc was of League design and recent manufacture, the sort with a viewing window.

Ciarán's feet briefly tangled with the fast pallet's control pedestal, an accident, or so he hoped it appeared, as he twisted in the harness in response, his fingers brushing the roebuck's legs, and his gaze lowering, and scanning the controls, and scanning the face of the man inside.

"Imbecile!", the roebuck shouted, as Ciarán pulled his legs clear. The distinctive whine of a pulse rifle spooling up flooded the compartment, then the sharp click of the weapon's safety disengaging.

"Cease motion!" the other roebuck shouted and Ciarán didn't need to pretend to ignore him. He held his legs clear and his arms high, the muzzle of the pulse rifle pressed to his chest.

It felt as if all the blood had drained from his face, and pooled in his gut, which was already roiling from the Templeman translation, draining not simply because his life might end with a single trigger squeeze, but because his future as a merchant *had* just ended, the instant his gaze had washed across the face of the man inside the autodoc, and Ciarán realized that he didn't just recognize the man. He *knew* him. Ciarán wasn't going to make that Prix Canada connection. He wouldn't arrive at Unity Station in time for his Merchant Guild examination.

The roebucks retreated with the fast-pallet, shoving it through the hatch and working the hatch controls from the corridor.

No sooner had the hatch closed than Ciarán was out of his harness and at the hatch controls. He might be an idiot at the moment, but he was certain he was going to be a corpse soon, unless he unbelted and got to work. He tapped the controls and scrolled to the compartment lighting settings, scanning for the advanced feature icon.

Found it.

He committed the changes he wanted and retreated to his seat, pausing beside his bug-out bag for just an instant. His pair of Hardhands would even the odds considerably but not enough. He was getting out of here on brains alone or not at all. Most likely not at all, but there was a chance. *Always a chance.*

He belted in.

The grain merchant stared at him.

"Well," she said. "Are you going to explain your actions?"

He thought about it for a minute before answering.

The Leagueman Charles Newton wouldn't answer. He *couldn't*, not without revealing he was entirely a fiction.

And Freeman Ciarán mac Diarmuid *shouldn't*, not on a League vessel, under League control. Not with the embargo in force.

There was only one man for the job, so to speak, and he was nearly a stranger.

"Sure," he said, in Trade Common.

The Dread Dermot, Mercenary Warlord and Scourge of the Outer Reach, grinned. "I'll explain it all right now."

6

"This is largely conjecture at this point," Ciarán said, "But it's consistent with the facts in every way, and it answers a number of nagging questions I've struggled with for some time."

Every word of that was true, but he wasn't certain how much of what he knew needed saying, and how much the grain merchant would be interested in, other than the details pertaining to their present situation.

"That man in the autodoc is Ship's Captain Danny Swan, commander of Thomas Truxton's *Rose*, out of Trinity Station, Freeman Federation. He's been missing for some time, and both his employer and his family are concerned, and willing to pay a considerable sum for his safe return."

"And you've been tracking him," the grain merchant said. "Because that's what tractor mechanics do."

He laughed. "You mean my utilities? The disguise matches my League non-resident identification, thought I may be putting on airs. I'm listed as a manual laborer on the rolls, but I feel like I would have risen up the ranks had I stayed with the work. And if you had a tractor I *could* fix it, provided it was ancient, and if not, I could at least hang in with the conversation, and talk a convincing game."

"So you're a bounty hunter."

"A friend of the family. Captain Swan was last seen alive in the Prescott Grange Station brig, shortly before the station fell."

"And you thought he went down with the station."

"I didn't, because I know for certain he was no longer on the station when it fell. Therefore—"

"How do you know that?"

"I know some people who were there at the time, and they told me he'd been released."

"Released to whom?"

"His crew, supposedly, but according to eye witnesses he was simply released from his cell and told to head for the docking ring. After which he disappeared. *And so*, since Swan is a Truxton captain, and there weren't any Truxton vessels listed in the area, I assumed he'd died in the incident, or been abducted again."

"Again?"

"He'd been taken captive while on holiday, and transported to Huangxu space, after which he escaped, and made his way to Prescott Grange. Hearing that news, the family thought him safely out of Huangxu hands."

"Why would anyone abduct a Freeman captain and take him to Huangxu space?"

"Didn't you get a look at him just now?"

"The autodoc was tilted away from me."

"He's the emperor's cousin."

"I didn't know there was a Freeman emperor."

Ciarán chuckled. "There are thousands of Freeman emperors. But I mean to say Danny Swan is the Huangxu emperor's cousin, and he's after taking the spire."

"What does *that* mean?"

"He has taken the Freeman Oath, and he wore the pendant

---

spire earring, in public, after which, when the Huangxu Eng caught him, they hacked off his ear, and paraded him in shackles from station to station. I expect there's still a public execution to be broadcast once they get their hands on him again."

"You're certain it's him."

"The autodoc indicated the patient inside had healed, and the man in there was yet missing an ear." And Ciarán had spent countless hours watching the video over and over again, of Danny Swan and the man he now knew as Hector Poole, on Peaceful Dawn Platform.

The man in the autodoc was definitely Danny Swan or a hound made from his pattern. Ciarán felt certain it was Swan.

The grain merchant glanced toward the hatch. "Who are these people, then, and what do they want?"

Ciarán grinned. "Good question. I thought, at first, they were Huangxu troops, but their weapons—"

"Ancient," she said. "OM-19s and DK-44s. Obsolete when my father was a cadet. But the bang sticks—"

"I have a theory about those. I hope I don't have to test it. Anyway, I think they're mercenaries or pirates, and while I'm not a bounty hunter—"

"They are."

"I think so." And after they'd found Swan, they were caught up in the system-wide gun battle. Lost their ship, or just their Templeman drive control. They must have been hiding out, possibly in one of the emergency survival stations he'd identified on his initial survey of the system weeks ago. Now the emergency was over and order being restored. It was only a matter of time until they were discovered. This was the last ship out before the Navy arrived in force to rebuild. A solitary troop transport, deadheading, almost, with minimal crew and a handful of passengers.

It was the sort of chance he would take, if he'd found

himself in the same situation. Success would depend entirely on nerve and the cohesiveness of the crew. Nerve they clearly had. But cohesiveness? *Not so much.* "Danny Swan is a prize, no doubt. One big enough to stir up dissent in the ranks."

"You mean the tall one."

"You saw it too. I think he's fixing to challenge the decantation order in a big way."

"What does *that* mean?"

"He's *junior* in the command structure to the golden hind, and it chafes. It wouldn't normally occur to him to do anything about it, but this is a big enough contract to reorder the dynamics of the company—if they can pull it off. If he's the one who turns over Danny Swan he'll get the credit. The roebucks are already recruited. I couldn't say about the other stags."

"What's a roebuck?"

"The guards they left with us. Smaller, with smaller racks."

"You mean the way they look like people with animal heads."

"With *deer* heads. The roe deer, it's a different species from your red deer. And about that, the way they appear. It's clear they fear being tagged and indexed, else they'd have dropped the fields once they were safely onboard and in superluminal space."

"I wouldn't know."

"Well, I do know. They're hiding something, but hiding it not all that well. Those fancy dress generators are kid's toys, and I have a friend who's a spoon merchant, and he'll stir it if it can be stirred. One of the gags he invented was what you saw me messing with just now, at the lighting controls. I switched the refresh frequency on the overheads to scanning mode. The costume generators are fixed frequency, so—"

"We'll be able to see through them."

"Should be able to, now and then. And if we can see their eyes—"

"We can aim between them."

"We could do that, too. But I was thinking we could tell if our arguments were getting through to them."

"What arguments?"

"Do you not know who Thomas Truxton is? Have you not heard of his flagship, the *Rose*?"

"I've heard the names."

"The man could *buy* the Hundred Planets if they were for sale. And Danny Swan isn't just some family-ship pilot. He's Truxton's most senior officer, and his second-most trusted advisor."

"And you work for Truxton."

"Not in a million years would I work for that man. But for the right price? I'd sell him something I had."

"You're going to make the pirates a better offer for Swan. On spec."

"I'm going to try."

"And if that doesn't work?"

"I'm still thinking about it."

"How about this idea," she said. "If it looks like you're not getting through to them you just keep talking and leave the rest to me."

"I could do that, if I knew what you had in mind."

"I'm not sure I trust you."

"That's because you don't know me."

"I'm not sure I want to know you, Mr..."

"Dermot. Leprous Brothers' *Impossible Bargains*. Out of Freeport Station."

"Freeport Station. Never heard of it."

Unsurprising, since I just invented it. "It's new. A work in progress, you might say, Ms..."

"Ellis. Mary Ellis. Geologist. Presently unemployed."

"This could be your lucky day, Ms. Ellis. I happen to be hiring. What do you say?"

"You couldn't afford me. Suppose we just fly in formation and see where that takes us."

"Suits."

She glanced toward the hatch.

So did Ciarán.

When it opened he wished he hadn't.

7
_____

A pair of League warrant officers stood framed by the hatch coaming. One flinched as she was shoved into the compartment. The other wobbled, and dripped blood onto the deck from a weeping head wound. She nearly fell as she was shoved forward. A veil of blood obscured her features. A pair of stags gripping bang sticks followed them into the compartment. The hatch closed as the golden hind strode in behind them.

The stags shoved the League pilots roughly to their knees.

"Do not struggle. Take your seats," the golden hind said. "Do as you are told and no further harm will come to you."

One of them did as ordered. The bloodied one did not.

"There is always a thick one," the hind said. "Do you desire more instruction, pilot?"

The woman turned to stare at the hind, her face a mask of blood. "Konstantine, Helen. Chief Warrant Officer, Service number seven four—"

"I've explained this twice already. We're not bound to any military protocol. Look." The golden hind switched off her own disguise, and motioned for the stags to do so as well. "No uniforms. No insignia. No rules. Just people with weapons. People you are making angry. I don't want to hurt you—"

"Then don't," Ciarán said. "Don't hurt her. Pilot, take your seat."

Konstantine shook her head. Her gaze focused as she seemed to realize that there were others in the compartment. She blinked, her eyes flashing white in a mask of red. "Karen? What are you doing here?"

"He's living to fight another day," the grain merchant said. "As we all should. Now take a seat, spacer, and await further orders."

Konstantine turned her head and blinked again. "Admiral Solon?"

"My mother," the grain merchant said. "She would advise you do the same."

Konstantine hesitated, glancing from face to face. One of her pupils showed larger than the other.

The grain merchant bellowed. "Strap in, spacer!"

"Sir!" Konstantine levered herself into a seat, fumbling with the strapping.

Ciarán's fingers found the harness latch as he began to rise. "There are field dressings in my luggage, Great Lady."

A bang stick rapped his knuckles.

The golden hind towered over him. "Keep it planted, Karen." She stared down at Ciarán. "Fang."

One of the stags answered. "Captain."

"Search the bags."

"Already on it," the second stag said, as he dumped the contents of Ciarán's bug-out bag onto the deck. A dozen Huangxu field dressings flopped out, packaging crinkling, followed by the rest of the gear he'd been lugging about for years.

"That is odd," the golden hind said.

Ciarán shrugged. "I like to be prepared."

"Not the contents of your bag," she said. "The fact that a League tractor repairman speaks Huangxu Eng." Her gaze met his. "Speaks it with a Celestial Palace accent."

The one called Fang dumped the grain merchant's bag beside the heap of Ciarán's gear, a dozen jewelry cases of various sizes and shapes, along with three large transparent sacks of uncut gems.

"That is also odd," the golden hind said.

"I also like to be prepared," the grain merchant drawled.

"So it appears. You learned your Huangxu in school?"

"Prison."

"Very good. It suits you. Zhao."

"Captain," the second stag said.

"Slap a field dressing on the stubborn cow."

"Already on it," Fang said.

Zhao hoisted the sacks full of gems. "The Admiral—"

"Will wish to argue for a share," the golden hind said. "Secure those, and leave the rest."

8

C iarán watched the pair as they worked and it was clear why they had chosen the disguises they had. Their utilities were uniformly dusty red, and their great height impossible to otherwise disguise. Pure-blooded Huangxu Eng, they seemed to bend like towering derricks to their work, the bags of gemstones disappearing into the lashed-down head compartment.

Helen Konstantine flinched as the field dressing draped across her scalp, and humped about for a while, muttering, before settling down with a sucking sound.

The golden hind watched in silence. Her utilities, like theirs, were unusually form-fitting for Huangxu issue, hers a dull gold that lapped her limbs and left little to the imagination.

He doubted she had pockets, but she did sport a belt, from which dangled various items, including a razor gun, and a handheld, and what he had at first glance thought was a bang stick. Upon closer inspection, however he was now fairly certain that the discipline rods they each carried weren't terror weapons, but an earlier stunner-only version of the device the bang stick had evolved from.

There was one simple test to determine if he was right. He and Mrs. Amati had trained with the stunners, and unlike a bang stick, they had a removable power supply, one an opponent might dislodge in a hand-to-hand engagement.

According to Amati only a fool would get close enough to an enemy to work that trick. In pitched combat, however, heroes and fools were often indistinguishable. Taking a strike for the squad was slightly less frowned upon than jumping on a grenade, but she'd seen both done. Standing by and letting your buddies get slaughtered was not an option.

So they practiced every way one might be set upon, with every weapon Amati had collected over the years, and inevitably Ciarán would fail. And inevitably Amati would hold out her hand, pull him to his feet, square off against him, and say what she always said. *Do it again.*

Some grenades needed jumping on, some could be kicked, and others picked up and hurled. And he knew which now, just as he knew just where one touched a stunning rod to eject the power supply. And if it came to it, how to grip a bang stick, take the hit, and fall, tangling the striker up and taking them out of the fight.

But only a hero or fool would do that, Amati had said. *Do this instead.*

He had felt a stabbing pain then, in the meat of his thumb, and had glanced down to his hand grasping the stunner, and Amati had opened her palm to show him the tiny blowgun dart she'd palmed, and he had glanced at his thumb, and the pinprick dot of blood there, and that was the last he had remembered.

Amati was a huge fan of the blowgun and he knew it. He thought of the device as a ranged weapon. It didn't occur to him that it was simply a dart delivery mechanism, and that he possessed two such additional mechanisms dangling from the ends of his arms.

He scrubbed his palm across his face and groaned. Amati crouched beside him and poked his chest with a finger, directly above his heart. *Turn this off.* She tapped him on the forehead. *Turn this on.*

And with that she diagnosed his problem completely. That was a practice round, what Amati called a sleepy dart, and not the real deal murder weapon. And he thought, or more accurately, didn't think, but *felt*, that one didn't use deadly force against someone with a stunner. Unless it turned out it wasn't a stunner, but a bang stick, which was equally stupid thinking, because in a real fight there wasn't any difference. Once stunned he'd be defenseless against anything, including a bang stick strike.

Amati helped him to his feet. She squared his shoulders and told him what he already knew. *I can't make a warrior out of you.*

She kicked his legs until they were a shoulder's width apart.

Only you can.

She handed him the stunner rod and marched across the compartment with murder in her eye.

Do it again.

And this time, imagine you're a sleeping mong hu.

Ciarán chuckled, and did as she asked. And that *worked*.

With that one sentence Amati reframed everything he struggled with. She put his doubts and regrets into a context he could survive. One he could embrace without sorrow.

He was surprised she knew that old Freeman saying.

What do you call a man who pokes a sleeping mong hu?

A corpse.

That story *persisted* because it was true. Few things appeared more peaceful than a slumbering mong hu. And they slept so soundly because the price of waking them was both certain and high.

If he wished to live a peaceful life out here in the wider world, he would need to be like the mong hu. He would need to become enough like the mong hu *that it showed.*

He hoped that it showed now, even while strapped to a crash seat, and that these people would not force him to do something they would regret.

He ran his gaze over the Huangxu Eng captain. She seemed his age, perhaps a little younger. Nearly pretty, but for the tight set of her jaw and the hard glint in her eyes. She stood close enough to him that he could feel the heat coming off her.

When he'd become entangled with the roebuck earlier he'd pickpocketed him, and stolen his knife. Seamus had shown him how, years ago, and there wasn't a better teacher alive. Not when it came to street crime.

He could take his seat and wait to see how events played out.

Or he could end her life, here and now.

The choice, and the responsibility, was entirely hers.

He inhaled her scent.

He knew which choice he preferred.

She glanced at him, and caught him studying her.

She took a step back, and glared. "Avert your gaze."

"A thousand pardons, Great Lady." He dipped his brow, and when he chose to, glanced away.

———————

9

S he might have said more if the hatch hadn't cycled. The tallest stag shoved Danny Swan into the compartment, then followed after him, the pair of roebucks trailing like breakbulk carts behind a docking-ring tractor.

Danny Swan remained upright, but only just.

The hatch remained open.

The golden hind's gaze narrowed as her voice lashed out. "You were told to guard the prisoners."

The hull shuddered.

"Drop separation," the grain merchant said.

She meant that a drop module had launched from the hull.

The hull shuddered again.

And again.

"We're in superluminal space," Ciarán said. There was nowhere for the modules to go.

The tallest stag chuckled. "The prisoners won't notice."

"Once a war criminal, always a war criminal," the grain merchant drawled.

"You recall my voice," the tallest stag said. "I am honored."

"Hardly. I recognized your stench," the grain merchant said.

The frequency scan trick had worked, and for an instant their disguises had grown nearly transparent. Ciarán would have to thank Seamus for that trick next time he saw him. *If there was a next time.*

"No wonder you disguise your face," the grain merchant said. "You're even uglier than I remember." She leaned back in her seat. "I'd say you looked stupider as well, but I think we both know that's an impossibility."

"Yet here you are. My captive again."

"The implied failure in that statement amuses me," the grain merchant said. "Why would you think this time any different than the last?"

"Because this time you are *alone*, Maris Solon."

The tallest stag dropped its disguise, and the roebucks did the same. They were all three Huangxu though only the tallest appeared Eng. The roebucks were physically similar to the Iron Fist mercenaries in Ciarán's accidental army. The tallest stag was entirely a new class of being in his experience, as if someone had taken the lithe elegance of the imperial Eng and *coarsened* it. His torso, his limbs, even his neck were thicker, corded with muscle, his brow lower, his eyes closer set, as if someone had crossed an Eng with a bear. He appeared far older than any Eng Ciarán had met. While his hair had not whitened it had grayed at the temples. He stood as if he owned the deck and everyone on it.

"It's a customer service dispute," Ciarán muttered. "Not an usurpation of the decantation order."

And the customer had just murdered some unknown number of passengers. He glanced at the golden hind. Her jaw worked, her eyes black diamond.

Not only that, but either the customer was mistaken, or the grain merchant had lied to him about her identity. She'd called herself Mary Ellis. And now it seems she might be someone called Maris Solon, a name he'd heard but couldn't place. And judging by her duffel contents she wasn't even a grain merchant. More like a gem merchant, which didn't make much sense in the torn-up wreckage of Prescott Grange space.

"You know this person," the golden hind said.

"An old enemy," the tallest stag said. "Once again in my power."

"Our arrangement was for one locate and retrieval."

"We will amend the contract. I wish to keep this one as well."

"And for the murder of prisoners? How will we amend the contract for that?"

"They are the enemy."

"They were *my* prisoners."

"They were *the enemy*. Now they are not. An accident will occur. A loss of all hands. No one will know."

"*I* will know! My *crew* will know!"

He scratched his chin. "That is true."

"Listen to me. We are *businesspeople*. In order to prosper we must prove *trustworthy*. I gave *my word* in exchange for cooperation. We cannot profit if every future boarding action devolves into a fight to the death. And supposing we might find ourselves captive one day. What will our fate be then, if it is known we deceive and murder those prisoners who trust our word?"

"You will be feared."

"Excellent. They will etch that on my grave marker. Captain Wing was a fearsome liar."

"Lieutenant Shi isn't a believer in grave markers," the grain merchant said. "The best you might hope for is a small plaque near the airlock controls."

"*Admiral* Shi," the largest stag said.

"Like I believe that," the grain merchant said. "An admiral commanding a mercenary crew, one without a vessel, and making a cockup of that?"

"He is an admiral," the golden hind said. "But he is not in command."

"I *paid* you to do a job," Shi said. "That makes me in charge."

"That job was nearly done," Wing said. "Done *my* way, without a single casualty."

"With honor," the grain merchant said.

Wing's dark eyes blazed. "Indeed."

"Honor has no value for those with none," the grain merchant said.

Ciarán understood what the grain merchant attempted. She made a mistake, however. It was too soon. One needed to foot the wedge before driving it home. She rushed forward where a merchant captain would wait. Plant the seed. Give it time to sprout. When the stalk took leaf, it would appear to be a miracle of self-invention. An argument pressed prematurely was as welcome as an invasive weed, and as likely to be uprooted.

Ciarán blurted out the first thing that popped into his head. "Who was it that launched the drop modules?"

Under any other circumstance his booming question would have been a mistake, but it seemed to have precisely the effect he desired. Shi's piercing gaze switched to him.

"One presumes there is a pilot at the helm," Ciarán said. "And there are six of you here, and that makes inauspicious seven. There must be a fortunate eighth. An accomplice previously aboard. Perhaps even several accomplices."

Shi's gaze narrowed as he peered down his nose at Ciarán. "The pilot launched them."

Ciarán nodded, as if pretending to understand. "Then who is piloting the vessel, Great Lord?"

"The autopilot is engaged."

"Oh." Ciarán grimaced. "Then who is minding the autopilot, Great Lord?"

"Idiot," Shi said. His gaze washed about the compartment, finally settling on the objects littering the deck. "What is this?"

"The contents of the prisoners' luggage," Wing said.

Shi kicked one of the field dressings. The wrapping crinkled and Ciarán imagined the dressing inside muttering, begging to be allowed to serve such a great lord.

"Those are expensive, Great Lord. Very difficult for this one to obtain." Ciarán avoided the grain merchant's angry gaze. It seemed quite clear to him that she was neither a grain merchant, nor a gem merchant, nor any other sort of merchant but, rather, an imposter. She possessed a layman's understanding of trade without the patience learned only through experience.

"These cases." Shi pointed at the jeweler's boxes emptied from the grain merchant's duffel. "What do they contain?"

"Jewelry, I presume," Wing said. "We were about to conduct an inventory when you arrived."

Shi toed through Ciarán's belongings. "Trash." When he kicked a signal green Academy Muscle shirt the corners of two books peeked out from beneath the fabric. "Trash wrapped in trash."

"Perhaps not," Wing said. Paper books are rare. Some are quite valuable."

"Look at him," Shi said. "Does he look as if he owns anything of value?"

"Close your eyes when he speaks," Wing said. "He might have learned his words at the emperor's knee." She ran her gaze over him, frowning. "This man is more than he appears."

Ciarán wished they would all close their eyes, all except Danny Swan. The Truxton Captain had lost some of the glazed look he'd worn upon entering the compartment and now seemed reasonably alert. Ciarán doubted that any of those in the compartment other than Swan and Konstantine had ever seen Freeman hand cant, but he couldn't be certain about the mercenaries. He signed to Swan, who didn't notice at first, but who quickly caught on. The idea that he had an ally seemed to inflate Swan, and when he cleared his throat, he stood taller and spoke clearer than Ciarán had hoped he might.

"He is a Freeman merchant, and matchmaker for our family. My sister sent him to restore balance for the People, in the tradition of the Mong Hu."

Shi snorted. "Min Zhi chose this planet-born trash to contend with me?"

"Agnes, she is named now. And she did not choose him. Tradition dictates. Likewise, she did not know it would be you in debt to us. You should listen to him and see what he proposes. Balance might yet be restored without bloodshed."

Shi grinned. "That would be disappointing."

"Your logic eludes me," Swan said. "As it always has."

"Logic is a crutch for children." Shi stalked closer to Ciarán, elbowing Wing out of his path.

Wing did not seem to appreciate that. Her brows knitted together like storm clouds colliding.

Shi glared down at Ciarán. "Does my logic elude you, *laji*?"

"Somewhat, Great Lord." Ciarán said. "Did you murder the prisoners before ejecting the drop modules? Or do you expect them to die as a result of ejecting the drop modules?"

"What difference would that make?" Wing said. "Either way they are dead."

"Perhaps not, Great Lady." Ciarán said. "Some might survive the ejection impulse load. These crash harnesses are quite stout, and the latches unique. They seem over-engineered for shipboard use."

"They are designed for troops in exoskeletal armor," Shi said.

"Unlikely, Great Lord. Examine their range of adjustment." Ciarán tugged his harness tighter to demonstrate. "The grain merchant is much smaller than any exo. Yet the harness fits her snuggly. This module, at least, is designed to accommodate spacers in utilities. To accommodate them under higher loads than a troop transport could generate on in-system drives alone."

"Grain merchant?" Wing said.

"The woman seated across from me, Great Lady. She seemed a grain merchant to me when I first sighted her. As her identity seems to remain in question I have yet to amend my original assessment." Ciarán forced a frown onto his face. "We were never formally introduced."

"There is no question," Shi said. "That woman is Maris Solon, a senior officer in the LRN and Columbia Station royalty. If she had simply been one or the other, I might have kept her."

Maris Solon chuckled. "Don't look so glum. A dozen war criminals in exchange for a midshipman? I'd say the Hundred Planets got the long end of the stick on that one."

"Perhaps so. But we were making such *progress*, you and I."

Ciarán didn't like the look on the grain merchant's face. She seemed ready to do something out of spite and desperation. Something unsurvivable.

"I've heard that name," he blurted out. "Maris Solon."

He had, and recently.

"Of course you have," Maris Solon said. "I started a war."

"Oh," Ciarán said. "You are the *Defiant* woman?"

She chuckled. "That seems accurate."

Both Seamus and Macer had told him about her. From their descriptions he thought they were describing two different women. The only thing their stories agreed on was that she was a senior captain, one with a lot of shipboard seat time.

"So as a League captain you would know," Ciarán said. "About these ejected drop modules. They're powered, right?"

"Right."

"But they're not going anywhere, being in a Templeman bubble, one a little bigger than the hull."

"They'll remain just inside the bubble until we drop into normal space."

"And then what?"

"They'll follow whatever flight profile has been programmed into them."

"Unless overridden."

"Naturally."

"The transport vessel's pilot can alter the course."

"Theoretically. But it's normally the module commander who orders any course changes."

"So—"

Maris Solon shook her head, slowly. "Give it up, young man. You're right up to a point, but no one survived to pilot those modules."

"Someone might have," Ciarán said.

"They were dead before the hatch closed." Maris Solon looked him in the eye. "As I said. Once a war criminal, always a war criminal."

Maris Solon ran her gaze over Shi. "He likes to hear them beg."

10

Ciarán wasn't happy with the way Admiral Shi towered over him. There were several ways to change the situation but each of them seemed unacceptable to some degree.

He could quite easily unbelt and stand. He'd studied the crash belt latching mechanism in enough detail to release it quickly and surreptitiously, with just a minor amount of misdirection. But then he'd stand toe to toe with the man, and everything would be out in the open. If he believed this Maris Solon person then there would be an immediate physical confrontation with a sadist, one that would end with bloodshed. Most likely his own.

He could press his matchmaker claim, drawing out the discussion and bidding for time. But again, this would bring him in direct confrontation with Shi, and in this case, while still strapped into a crash seat with the man yet towering over him. Such relative positions presented the appearance of weakness on his part. He did not believe Shi would be able to overlook this. Any agreement they made would likely be one-sided against the Swans. And while Ciarán had offered to serve as matchmaker for Agnes Swan, in truth she hadn't agreed. He had little doubt she would back the claim, however, if it came to a court case, and any postdating of the intent documentation accepted with one eye closed, where the victim was Freeman and the perpetrator a Huangxu Eng war criminal.

Given the nature of the offense any match made would almost certainly involve a blood price. And extracting the price would require him to unbelt and stand without being murdered in the process.

He gazed up at Shi. He glanced at the roebucks. They remained alert, fingertips lapping the trigger guards of their ancient Oscar-mikes. Likely to overheat on full automatic but not while squeezing off a round or two into one oversized Free-man. In a scuffle with Shi they might not get involved for fear of hitting Shi with their fire. But all Shi needed to do was step back to prevent that. Thus Ciarán was likely to be murdered before he had his feet under him.

He'd taken the measure of those in the compartment before he'd begun orchestrating his cavalcade of convolutions. There were now four brain-twisting threads of bunkum occupying minds and adding to what was already a confused and distracting situation.

What about the ejected drop modules? *Do I need to be concerned?*

Is anyone really piloting the vessel? *Do I need to be concerned?*

What is a Freeman matchmaker, and what is he going to do? *Do I need to be concerned?*

Why is a tractor repairman carrying a lifetime supply of Huangxu field dressings and speaking with a Celestial Palace accent? *Do I need to be concerned?*

Of course, he had his own concerns crowding his mind. He had experience, however, at shoving such thoughts aside. There were a great number of what appeared to be coincidences begging for attention. *What is Danny Swan doing on this vessel? What is Helen Konstantine doing on this vessel? What is the woman who started the war between the Federation and the League doing on this vessel?*

If he were not familiar with the iron law of coincidences, he might yet be wasting time puzzling over matters that he could not control. Either they were bad coincidences, in which case he would discover how fate had shafted him in due time, or they were not coincidences at all, just the work of some unseen and provident hand; in which case he might profit from a friendly fortune and need only remain alert while actively searching for the hidden handle on the situation. And still be pumping air when it came time to grasp it.

He had already recruited Maris Solon to his cause. She had agreed to allow him to make his case with the mercenaries for the release of Danny Swan to Truxton. Of course, that had been before he'd discovered that the mercenaries' existing customer was also on board, and a homicidal maniac with a festering grudge against Swan—and also against Maris Solon.

Ciarán wondered if there was profit in having Shi transfer his ire to him. Perhaps Swan and Solon were delivered to him because they possessed some hidden resources he did not. Perhaps *he* was delivered to *them* because he possessed some hidden resources the others did not.

Such speculation inevitably proved pointless. One could not second guess providence or argue with fate. Better to keep his eye on the balls in play, and toss a few more into the air, and watch for the slightest pattern. A shape would emerge that he might exploit, even if he couldn't see it yet.

What he needed most of all was more allies, preferably ones with guns.

There was a way, but it wouldn't be easy. And even if he didn't pull the trigger spacers might die.

He glanced at Helen Konstantine. She was out cold, the

field dressing working its magic. The selfless and mewling creature draped across her forehead had been bio-engineered to serve. To give its life so that others might live.

The field dressing might well save Konstantine's life.

A life henceforth spent in a Huangxu prison camp.

Or more likely, one cut short by a razor gun to the back of the head, or a short walk out an airlock.

Ciarán took a deep breath.

Unacceptable.

He knew what he had to do.

11

"Well, Min Zhi's matchmaker?" Shi stared down at him. "Contend with me."

"Establishing balance depends, firstly, Great Lord, upon a true accounting of grievances. As I have witnessed nothing I would consider a grievance, I'm not certain balance can be restored by contending with you."

"No grievance, you say?"

"None worthy of comment, Great Lord. You arrived upon this vessel, at immense personal risk. You maintained Captain Swan's health, apparently as best as you might, in an autodoc of recent manufacture. You revived him and delivered him to me without prompting."

"*Delivered* him to you?"

"That was the agreement, Great Lord, was it not? Thus you have received payment from Truxton as agreed."

Shi snorted. "Payment? With what? Expired med packs?"

"Three sacks of uncut gems, Great Lord, for the delivery of Danny Swan to me. Untraceable, as agreed. We need now only agree on the price of transport to Freeman space." He paused for an instant, and smiled. "I am permitted to be generous in this matter."

Shi stared down at Ciarán. "You expect me to sell this traitor to you?"

"I understood you already had, Great Lord. Why else would your people accept payment on your behalf?"

"You paid my people."

"Ask them yourself, Great Lord."

Ciarán glanced at the golden hind. Captain Wing's face had grown ashen.

"That is a lie," she said. "It is all lies."

"Great Lady, I will not dispute you, but rather, allow the facts to speak for themselves."

"What facts?" Shi said.

"We were alone with your people for quite some time, while they unpacked the autodoc. Subsequent to that effort your people inspected our luggage and discovered the gems. They took possession of the gems. One presumes they did so upon your behalf. What other explanation can there be?"

Shi frowned. "I don't believe you."

"I don't ask you to believe me, Great Lord. The proof is hidden in the portable refresher."

Shi pointed at one of the roebucks. "Li. Look."

The man moved toward the portable head.

"Why would he need to look, Great Lord? Why does he not simply tell you what he did?"

"Li took these gems from you."

"I do not know his name, Great Lord. And he wore a mask. They both wore masks."

Ciarán watched Captain Wing's face. After a moment Wing spoke.

"Fang. See if this is true."

"It is not true," Li said.

"We will know soon enough," Wing said.

Fang entered the head and returned with two of the three bags, one in each hand.

"Explain this," Wing said.

Li glanced from face to face. "It is a lie."

"Zhao," Wing said.

An Oscar-mike barked.

And barked again.

12

C iarán lurched against the crash belts as the pair of Huangxu slumped to the deck. "You shot them!" He'd wanted to engineer an argument, not incite bloody murder.

"That is what we do with those who betray us," Wing said.

"Those were my personal guard," Shi said.

"Perhaps you should have paid them better." Wing turned her attention to Ciarán. "There was no arrangement to ransom the traitor. A side deal, perhaps, between two greedy servants and this Truxton. Do you truly believe Admiral Shi would sell you this man for three shabby bags of third-rate stones?"

"They are somewhat more than that," Maris Solon said. "You might wish to have your eyes examined."

"No offense was meant, Great Lady. Those were a down payment only," Ciarán said. "I am authorized to negotiate on the Merchant Lord's behalf. Surely agreement may be reached."

"One cannot put a price on justice," Wing said.

"The Emperor does, Great Lady. Admiral Shi himself has stated that prisoner exchanges have occurred. What is that, but pricing justice? What is one man's life worth, balanced against the needs of an empire?"

"Trade for a thief and a deserter? There could be no amount worth noticing."

"This man is neither of those, but a ship's captain, and trusted advisor to a wealthy merchant lord."

"How wealthy?"

"Truxton fields a fleet of vessels second only in number to the League Navy. He has agents on a thousand worlds."

Wing snorted. "That is an exaggeration."

"It isn't," Maris Solon said. "If anything, it's an understatement."

"Then why haven't I heard of this Truxton?"

"Doubtless you have, Great Lady. He trades in the Hundred Planets under the 'Dustman' service mark." Ciarán reached into his pocket slowly and retrieved a pen and pad. He unscrewed the pen's cap. "I will draw the mark for you."

"I know it." Wing glanced at Shi. "You hired us to retrieve a thief and deserter. Did you know this man was a rich man's captain?"

Ciarán touched Wing's sleeve. "Not any rich man's captain, Great Lady. The *personal* captain of the richest man in Freeman space. A lifelong comrade and confidant."

Wing's eyes blazed. "Is this so, Admiral?"

"What of it? He stole from me. He deserted his command."

"Such knowledge would have certainly altered the price of recovering him."

"That's why he didn't tell you," Maris Solon said.

Shi's handheld squawked. He touched the controls. "Pilot."

"Admiral, we have a problem."

"What is it?"

"It's easier to show than to explain."

Shi took a long, deep breath. "Very well. I'm on my way."

The League pilot unbelted and stood.

"Sit," Fang said.

"The first officer is Shi's inside man," Maris Solon said. "You really didn't think a squad of carbine-toting grunts could steal a League military vessel, did you?"

"Captain?" Zhao said.

"Of course I knew," Wing said. "I chose to withhold the information. We needed to act as if we were operating without inside help."

Maris Solon chuckled. "Try it again, spacer, but with conviction this time."

"I am confused," Ciarán said. "Great Lord—"

The hatch cycled and both Shi and the League pilot stepped through.

The compartment annunciator sounded seconds later. "Fang?"

"Yes, Admiral?"

"Bind the deserter and Maris Solon. Kill the rest."

13

"Fang," Captain Wing said. "Belay that order."

Fang chuckled. "Yes, Captain."

One of the roebucks groaned.

A flick of the wrist and Ciarán was out of his seat, the crash harness dropping away as he rose. He took two steps before anyone noticed. He bent and scooped up a pair of field dressings one-handed. He straightened and took a step toward the wounded men.

A bang stick poked him beneath the jaw.

Wing blocked his path, staring him in the eye. "Did I tell you to stand?"

"You didn't. Now if you'll step aside, I'll see to the wounded."

"You didn't, *Great Lady*."

"That's what I meant to say. Now if you'll just move aside—"

"Take your seat."

"I will, once I've seen to the—"

"You will obey me. Instantly."

"I'd like nothing better." He would obey her under any other circumstance. There wasn't any reason not to obey her, and a thousand reasons to do so. There would be a time to defy her and this wasn't that time.

He'd expected an argument, stunners, restraints, an interrogation, something time consuming and emotionally charged. Time for him to think, to prod, to remove entropy from the situation, inject chaos, add uncertainty, time to witness the path forward emerge from the fog of truths and half-truths he'd pumped into the compartment: hidden resonances revealed, buried motivations indicated, undetected fractures to be exploited, secret desires to be fueled, anything. Everything might prove a handle, so long as he kept them talking.

He hadn't expected cold blooded murder and a walkout.

The walkout he could deal with. But he'd promised himself. If it came to killing, he wouldn't back away from it. But he wasn't killing anyone by error or omission ever again.

"I'm not trying to save them for their own sake. It's just, I might need them again, later." He reached up and tapped the stunner that looked like a bang stick. Tapped it *right there.*

The power supply fell out.

Wing nodded. "I understand." She kept the stunner jammed against his flesh.

Ciarán swallowed. "I didn't hear the power supply hit the deck."

"That's because it's landed in my free hand." Wing smiled. "I felt I might need it again."

"Later, you might need it, you mean."

Wing chuckled. "Then, too."

14

He'd been stunned before. Mrs. Amati had insisted upon it. She said he needed to know what it felt like so that he'd know how to deal with the aftereffects when it happened for real. And it would happen, not if, but when, so it was better he be prepared.

He hadn't liked the experience and he wouldn't have agreed to it if he'd known what it would feel like beforehand. She'd recorded the strike so he could watch himself drop like a felled tree, and minutes later, begin to twitch on the deck, groan, and attempt to clamber uselessly to his feet.

Amati had chuckled, as she watched him, watching himself. *Don't do any of that. Just lay there, silently.*

He'd said he wasn't sure he could do that, and she said, *Let's see*, and stunned him again.

He was able to do that—the thought that if he didn't he might be stunned again largely responsible for his success.

Amati crouched over him and tapped him with the stunner. *Does it feel like you can get up now?*

He wanted to tell her that it did, but he remained silent.

He didn't move a muscle for what felt like forever.

That had been bad, but nothing compared to a Huangxu stunner. It had felt like his brain had instantly inflated to three times its normal size and slammed against the inside of his skull. He wanted to scream but no words came out. He expected to lose consciousness, but he hadn't. He muscles tried to writhe but couldn't. It was as if his consciousness had been ripped free from his body and had no control over what might as well have been a corpse, but a deaf, dumb, and blind corpse that remained minutely aware of every painful insult to its screaming undead nerves.

He was lifted and wrestled into a seat. Strapped in. Poked.

He had no idea when the effect would wear off, or if it ever would. He could easily imagine how the bang stick could have evolved from this. He felt trapped inside his own skull, unable to communicate and incapable of escaping, a prisoner of a fleshy cell he couldn't control. He felt a well of panic open inside him. If he let it grow it would engulf him.

He forced him mind to think. To analyze. To deduce.

Logic might be a child's crutch, as Admiral Shi had said, but he would lean on any prop he could find, so long as it meant he could stand the pain just one instant longer.

There remained a missing piece, one that had not yet been turned over. The seeming coincidences were too densely packed together inside this hull for it to be a matter of natural occurrence alone. Someone had arranged this unconventional collision of conflicting interests.

But to what end?

His mind screamed whenever he stopped thinking. He wondered if he'd emerge into the world again, and if he did, would he be the same man or an insane shadow, suitable only for an asylum of the criminally maimed, and an endless burden to his family and those he loved.

There was no profit in such speculation. He needed to remain focused. Focused on who, or what, had chosen to derail him from his path. It seemed unlikely now that he would make it to Unity Station in time for the Merchant's examination.

After a very long while he began to hear voices. He thought they were imaginary at first. Several people, talking about someone named Karen.

He wanted to open his eyes, but he didn't dare.

He wanted to twitch a finger, but he didn't dare.

He simply sat there and listened.

He realized, after a moment, that one of the speakers was Helen Konstantine. And it all snapped into focus. They weren't talking about anyone named Karen.

They were talking about him.

15

"That absolves me," Konstantine said. "I was worried that it was me that would be the death of Karen. As it is it'll be a mercy for him. I've seen what your devil sticks do to a human being."

"It is a stunner," Wing said. "He will suffer no permanent effects."

"Who is this Karen," a man's deep voice said.

"Karen Mack Dermot," Konstantine said. "Merchant apprentice off *Quite Possibly Alien*."

"I see," the man said. "That is how this man and my sister became acquainted."

The man speaking was Danny Swan.

"Became acquainted? Scraped hulls is more like it," Konstantine said. "Though Eefah tells me the two of them have aligned courses since I separated from the crew."

"That would be Aoife nic Cartaí," Danny Swan said. "Merchant captain."

"That's right. It's a good thing we're all going to die, else there'd be hell to pay in the Hundred Planets. Two Nick Carty wars at once, if it came out this bit of fluff bang-sticked Eefah's apprentice."

"It is not a bang stick," Wing said. "It is a stunner."

"Right," Konstantine said. "And I'm the dowager mother."

"I haven't surrendered hope of rescue yet," Swan said.

"That's because you don't know what I know," Konstantine said. "There's more than a bit of trouble on the bridge."

Maris Solon cleared her throat. "What have you done, Pilot?"

"I can see now you're not Admiral Solon," Konstantine said. "I apologize for the mistake."

"You're not the first to make it. Now—"

"You look exactly like her."

"She *is* well preserved for her age."

"Right. I mean, sorry. You look now like she did, years ago. When she addressed the fleet cadets."

"I knew what you meant, Pilot."

"I figured you did. You don't remember me, do you?"

"You seem familiar."

"We were on a joint special operations deployment years ago. You jocked that little superluminal gunboat."

"*Durable*," Solon said.

"Right. I thought it was a stupid name, but it somehow managed to get in and get out. I was certain we'd bite it during the extraction. I'd never seen such a shot up piece of junk in all my years, and that's what I told the refit master at Brasil Yards when I saw what was left of that hull, afterwards." Konstantine chuckled. "I asked him if there were any survivors."

"'That's the horse you rode in on', he says.

"That was a dread surprise to me. I'd spent the entire outbound in the piece-of-shite arguing with the Dapper LT about his dirt-nap-inspiring intel. It was just the two of us and eight body bags in there and it was a hot boost, no lie. I think I would have fragged him if I'd had the cavalry call sign on speed dial, and not stored in his noggin."

"That was a long time ago," Solon said.

"My first down-and-back for real," Konstantine said. "You never forget your first."

"I suppose not," Solon said.

"I saw him the other day," Konstantine said. "The Dapper LT. First time since I busted his nose on the Brasil Station arcade. He's a major now."

"You saw the intelligence officer from that cruise," Solon said. "You saw him recently."

"A week ago yesterday," Konstantine said. "On Sizemore Station. It's funny, finding you here, and you being the boss of that hull."

"Not funny. Odd, perhaps," Solon said. "Describe your conversation."

"Well... I was off duty, and on the arcade, and a having a beer with some mates. Today was to be my second-to-last boost in uniform, and it was sort of an informal mustering out party, and he just shows up, big as Zeus and twice as haughty, if you recall the man."

"I recall him. What did he want?"

"He said he'd heard I was on the station and that I'd be heading for Prescott and would I deliver some documents for him."

"Documents."

"A data crystal."

"Deliver them to whom?"

"Eefah Nick Carty. I wasn't aware that *Quite Possibly Alien* had already boosted, so I told him fine, I would. It wasn't for him, but Eefah I agreed."

"That was the extent of your conversation?"

"Almost. Your ship came up. *Durable*. Sort of in a sideways manner, though. He said they were auctioning off a bunch of government surplus and that old hulk was in the lot. He asked if I wanted to go in halfsies with him, now that I was soon to be unemployed.

"I told him I'd been happily employed, right up until the Navy recalled me to active duty, and all just to mess with me, and I'd go back to being happily employed, and he could shove his smirking face and his halfsies up his own—"

"Where and when is this auction?"

"Oh. I don't know where. Brasil, I expect, if it's an active hull aged out. Or Sizemore, if it's in the reserve stockpile."

"When?"

"That I *do* know. He wrote it down on a napkin, but I'd remember it anyway, because it's my birthday."

"Which is?"

"Tomorrow, not that it matters anymore."

"Because?"

"Because once I realized we were being hijacked I reset the course and pegged the boards. We're dropping out of superluminal space one centimeter shy of Sizemore's tripwire. Two seconds later we'll be boosting at full military power directly toward the station. I've overridden the fail-safes."

"What?" Wing said. "No."

"Pegging the boards is fleet doctrine," Solon said. "It's survivable. Once we're in normal space—"

"Once in normal space," Konstantine said, "We're firing every unoccupied can at the station. It's not a full spread but enough to spin up the defensive grid."

"It will look like we're attacking the station," Wing said.

"For an instant it will," Konstantine said. "Then it will look like a smear of whatever's left after a hijacked troop transport and all its drop modules are slagged to glass."

"You can't do this," Wing said.

"It's already done," Konstantine said. "It just hasn't happened yet."

"But—"

"Listen," Konstantine said. "I am *this* close to being out. And the navy's been good to me, but it hasn't been great. I thought about it once I realized what was going on. Thought about it, for like a *total* of three milliseconds.

"No one is taking *my* vessel," Konstantine said. "Absolutely *no one.*"

"*Do not* mess with the fleet," Solon said.

"That is the law, sir," Konstantine said. "That is the ironclad law."

16

"You *will* undo this," Wing said.

"Make me," Konstantine said.

"It can't be undone," Maris Solon said. "Nothing short of a Templeman drive ejection can stop it."

Ciarán decided to risk moving the pinky on his left hand. *That worked.*

"You are returned to us," a male voice whispered beside him. Fang, or Zhao, he couldn't decide.

Ciarán wasn't certain how to respond.

"Do not speak," the man said. "Do not move. Simply listen."

Ciarán followed instructions. He wished Merchant Captain Aoife nic Cartaí was here as witness.

"We are amenable to an agreement. One that preserves life. If you choose to make such an offer and Wing refuses? Demand she put the decision to a company vote. If you understand me speak now. Admiral Shi returns."

Ciarán cleared his throat. He blinked, as the missing piece slid into place. "This Dapper LT. The one that is now a major." He glanced at Konstantine. "Is he a *Home Guard* major? Looks like a recruiting poster? Sounds like an unctuous popinjay? Never seems to say anything but won't shut up?"

Konstantine stared at him. They all seemed to stare at him.

"I don't know," she said. "What's a popinjay?"

"Parrot," Maris Solon said. "Showy feathers, always preening. Oily. Artificial. Glossy. Well meaning? Perhaps. Self-serving? Always."

"That is the Dapper LT," Konstantine said. "Can't get enough of himself and not afraid to advertise it."

Maris Solon chuckled. "They're all like that, you know. Aster's people."

"That's grand," Ciarán said. "And maybe useful to know later if we live that long. But right now, we're discussing one man, and I'd like to know what he called himself when you knew him."

"I still know him," Konstantine said.

"When you first met him, I meant to say. And henceforth."

"He never volunteered, but it came out later, during the inquiry." Konstantine said. "I wasn't there, but I heard about it."

"I was there," Maris Solon said. "As a material witness."

"You would have been," Konstantine said. "Watching it all go pear-shaped from orbit. There was nothing to see from inside the piece-of—"

"His name," Ciarán said.

"Poole," Solon said. "Hector Poole."

"I know that name," Danny Swan said.

"I figured you would," Ciarán said. "We have images of you with Poole on Peaceful Dawn Platform. He helped you escape."

"He did not help me at all. I was searching for a friend. A lover. She had gone missing. This man, Poole, said he knew where she was. She was not there. *He* was."

"Poole."

"No. I mean, yes, Poole was there, but in league with *him*. Admiral Shi."

"Poole handed you over to Shi?"

"He wanted me to stop looking. He said I was interfering. Getting in the way. That if I did not stop making inquiries he would make me stop. He said I risked her life. I did not believe him." Swan inhaled deeply. He slowly exhaled. "I could not *bear* to believe him."

"Wait," Ciarán said. "Which of them told you this? Poole or Shi?"

"Poole. The Leagueman betrayed me, and delivered me to my enemies. All to stop me searching for her."

"That is not entirely true," Fang said.

Swan leaned forward in his seat. "No?"

Fang locked gazes with Wing. "No."

"And why not?" Swan said.

"Because Fang also knows that man," Wing said.

17

"A man calling himself Hector Poole contacted the Mighty Eighty-Eight," Wing said. "Searching for news of a missing League woman. Fang manages such interactions with foreigners."

"We have worked with this man before," Fang said. "And—"

"You're the Mighty Eighty-Eight," Maris Solon said.

"What if we are?" Wing said.

Well, I expected you would be..." Solon scratched her eyebrow. "More... numerous."

"We were," Wing said, "Until the events at Prescott Grange. Our vessel was targeted and holed; the superluminal drive damaged. We had only begun abandoning ship when the containment sphere let go."

"Women and children first," Maris Solon said.

"Passengers and prisoners first," Wing said. "And I dislike like your intimations."

"Perhaps you'll like them more if I make them explicit."

"Who the hell is the Mighty Eighty-Eight," Konstantine said.

"A mercenary company," Maris Solon said. "Quite infamous. Quite expensive. Quite... amoral."

"The Eighty-Eight are not mercenaries," Ciarán said. "But let's stay on topic here. Fang, what wasn't true about what Captain Swan just said? Be precise. And the rest of you." Ciarán glanced from face to face. "No interrupting."

Fang nodded. "The falsehood is simply this. Admiral Shi could not be in league with Hector Poole because Shi has never met Hector Poole."

Danny Swan pressed forward against his seat's crash webbing. "Then how did Shi find me? How did he know of my quest?"

"Because the woman you searched for, Anastasia Blum, told him. The woman was there, on Peaceful Dawn Platform. The Admiral is entirely her vassal."

"Impossible," Swan said.

"I witnessed this," Fang said. "Anastasia Blum and the General were quite..."

"Intimate," Maris Solon said.

"Indeed," Fang said.

"I don't believe you," Swan said.

Ciarán felt as if he'd been gut-punched. It was entirely possible, what Fang had witnessed, but it wasn't Annie Blum who'd been in charge. He'd thought that with Vatya dead he'd be rid of her memory. That he had witnessed the worst she and Ixatl-Nine-Go could do to a human being.

"Hector Poole did not betray you," Fang said. "He paid the Eighty-Eight to deliver you to League space. And so we did."

"And Shi?" Swan said. "Did he pay you to return me to the Hundred Planets?"

"That sounds fairly mercenary to me," Maris Solon drawled.

"He did not," Fang said.

"Lies," Danny Swan said. "All lies."

"I believe him." Ciarán turned to Wing. "Prior to this..."

"This utter hull-rend, stem to stern?" Wing said.

"Prior to that. Were the Eighty-Eight acquainted with Admiral Shi?"

"He is Commandant of Detention. What reason would we have to interact with such a one?"

"By Detention you mean prisoner of war camps."

"I wouldn't call them camps," Wing said. "But facilities. All facilities where prisoners are... held."

"And Shi's relation to Captain Swan?"

"Swan's commanding officer. Swan's father fell out of favor with the emperor. His son was transferred to Shi's command, and his daughter... gifted to Shi."

"When was this?"

"Decades ago."

"Danny Swan would have been how old?"

"Seventeen, when he deserted and fled to the Federation. Such desertion remains a crime punishable by death."

"And his sister?"

"Min Zhi?"

"Agnes was nine," Danny Swan said. "It is a crime—"

"Indeed," Wing said. "It is a crime. The demands of honor—"

"I care *nothing* for honor," Swan said. "I *love* her. I could not witness her—"

"Savaged by a monster?" Maris Solon said.

"Thrown to a pack of wolves," Wing said. "We have a recording of Captain Swan's confession."

"Coerced confession," Swan said.

"That is not the language of coercion," Wing said. "It is the sound of righteous outrage."

"Besides Captain Swan and Maris Solon," Ciarán said, "Who else here knew Admiral Shi?"

It appeared no one did.

He turned to face Maris Solon. "You were Shi's prisoner?"

"Yes."

"And you knew him well?"

"I knew him... intimately. I was only a midshipman but senior officer in the camp."

"And?"

"Shi was under the impression that if he... humiliated me... I might..." She licked her lips. "I might..." She scrubbed her hands together. "You know, I don't know what he had in mind. All I know is that it didn't work. It would never have worked. What *these* people, what people like Shi find repugnant, amusing, disgraceful... We have very different standards on Columbia Station. I wasn't some frontier bumpkin. There was nothing he could do, not to me, in public, in private, nothing that I didn't find tedious, or irritating, at best. As for the others—"

"You weren't alone," Ciarán said.

"Never," Maris said. "We were in enemy hands, but we were not alone." She stared into the distance. "I was simply his favorite. The tallest poppy in the field."

Ciarán glanced at Wing. "Admiral Shi is under the impression that he has hired the Mighty Eight-Eight to return Danny Swan to him."

"He is under the impression he has hired mercenaries," Wing said. "With money."

"And Hector Poole?"

"He has paid the Mighty Eighty-Eight."

"Paid you for what?"

"To deliver Admiral Shi to Senior Captain Maris Solon," Fang said. "Upon her arrival in Prescott Grange system. Of course, that delivery was meant to happen weeks ago."

"When Admiral Shi returns he will expect to find Konstantine and me dead," Ciarán said.

"He expects to find all but Fang and the prisoners dead," Wing said.

"The Admiral believes he and I have a side agreement," Fang said.

Ciarán had wondered about that. "What will he do when he discovers his mistake?"

"We will see," Wing said.

Ciarán tore off a bit of his unused luggage tag and wadded it into a tiny adhesive ball. He snapped his fingers, flicking it toward the hatch control. It stuck to the bulkhead a centimeter above the control.

He tried again, killing time, four misses, bracketing the control.

"You are a very poor shot," Wing said.

Ciarán nodded. "So I've been told."

Wing moved toward the seat beside him. She sat with practiced grace, and belted in, her bangs brushing his cheek. She held out her hand, palm up. "Let me try."

He deposited six crumpled wads of tacky paper on her palm.

"Like this?" She sighted the target and snapped her fingers, her gaze directed downrange.

"Look down," Ciarán said.

The adhesive ball had adhered to her fingertip.

"Do it again," Ciarán said.

When their gazes met she nearly smiled. "You have acquired a master?"

"I have acquired a dozen masters."

"A weapons master, I mean."

"I have acquired a dozen weapons masters. Do it again," he said.

She did. The tiny ball landed on the deck.

"Knowledge is a weapon." he said. "Experience is a weapon."

"Words are a weapon." She tried again, and again failed.

"The right words, at the right time." He took her hand in his, adjusting her fingers. "Do it again."

"How do you know of us?" She snapped her fingers, her tacky missile adhering to the deck before the hatch. "Reload," she said.

He placed the pea-sized weapon upon her palm.

"I wanted to buy a mercenary company, so I did a great deal of research. The Mighty Eighty-Eight were the only company listed without a table of services and pricing schedule. I am intrigued by anomalies. I wanted to know if that was a mistake."

She snapped her fingers and smiled. She'd managed to adhere a spitball to the hatch. "Hire a company, you mean."

"Not hire. Purchase." He placed a new load on her outstretched palm. "I could find nothing in writing. So I asked around."

He'd discovered they were the Huangxu Eng equivalent of the Freeman Fianna, sons and daughters of the ruling elite. They organized like a mercenary company, but one with strict entrance examinations, both physical and mental, and one with the rolls capped at eighty-eight. According to Old, Ninth Cohort Captain of the Invincible Spear Bearers of Imperial Wrath, the Mighty Eighty-Eight were both deadly and unpredictable, hiring out half the year and mooching off one station after another the other half. The stationmasters could do nothing, because the Mighty Eight-Eight were too respected to turn away and too feared to chase off. They were the only mercenary company one could hire to fight the Hundred Planets military, because they were composed entirely of those callow youths who felt no filial attachment to the emperor.

According to Old, the Mighty Eighty-Eight could not be hired with money. One could, however, engage their interest by offering them *novelty*. They were exceptional at stern chases, neither flagging nor disengaging, though it was said if one could evade them for half a year they would admit, not defeat, but stalemate.

According to Ming, Chieftain of the Black Turtle Clan, the Mighty Eighty-Eight had outworn their welcome in the Original Hundred Planets, and given the current turmoil with the Eight Banners Empire, likely to find themselves unwelcome henceforth wherever they went. There remained a stubborn rumor that those elders who had once fought under the Eighty-Eight's banner in their youth now plotted a military coup, with the company itself acting as the tip of the spear.

The natives weren't so much concerned about the lingering spear-tip as they were about the Imperial troops increasingly billeted wherever one might expect the Eighty-Eight to alight for their off-season parasitism.

"Reload," she said.

He complied, and she looked him in the eye, her gaze locking with his, her eyes gleaming and fierce, as she snapped her fingers and flicked. He did not need to look to know that she had struck the control panel squarely in the center. She had been toying with him, there was nothing here for her, not anymore, nothing but the novelty of showing him up, of *besting* him, and now even that was gone.

"A lucky shot," she said. "Shall I try again, master?"

Ciarán dipped his hand into his pocket as the compartment hatch cycled. He glanced toward the hatch and *flicked*, his gaze returning to hers as a blowgun dart seemed to miss its target, Admiral Shi's jugular vein, and buried itself into the center of the sadist's left eye. Shi's forehead thudded against the deck. The League first officer he'd been using as a human shield wobbled on her feet, the Huangxu pilot cursing and doing his best to hold her upright.

Ciarán pressed a quartet of spitballs onto her palm. "Do it again." He closed her hand into a fist and unbelted. "Do it again. And again. Do it until you can miss the target by precisely three centimeters six times in a row."

Ciarán toed Admiral Shi onto his back and removed the dart. He yanked the bang stick from beneath the Admiral's belt. He'd seen the truth the instant his gaze had washed over the League first officer's slack-jawed face and spotted the seven red bang stick burns dotting her neck and jaw.

"Is he dead?" Maris Solon asked.

"It's a sleepy dart," Konstantine said. "You can tell by the color of the tail feathers."

"Can you?" Maris Solon said.

"I could use some help here," the Huangxu Eng pilot said. He had the League first officer by the waist and was holding her upright.

"Toss her in the corner," Konstantine said. "When they hang her, they'll prop her upright."

Ciarán took the woman's weight off the pilot and hoisted her into a crash seat. She was barely breathing. "What's her name?"

"Steyr," Konstantine said. "Omega Steyr."

Maris Solon nearly shouted. "The hell you say."

"Don't sound so surprised. The whole lot of that clan's rotten to the core, and they can hang me for saying so, if they can get to me in—"

Ciarán ripped open a field dressing and draped it across the wounds. He ripped open another and did the same.

"—sixteen hours, twenty-one minutes, and some seconds."

"Come on, Steyr," Ciarán muttered. "Hang in there."

"Don't waste your time," Konstantine said.

"I'm not wasting my time." He checked her pulse.

"We're all going to die anyway," Konstantine said.

"That's a given." There wasn't any cure for a bang stick strike. There wasn't any treatment. "I know nothing about this woman but her name. What would cause her to betray her

oath? Was it want of money? Was it a threat to her? To her
family? I can imagine a thousand different ways she could be
compelled to *appear* disloyal, and yet remain constant to her
family and friends. To her oaths and promises.

"We are traveling in a vessel awash with lies and misdirection.
If I'm going to assume *anything* about her, I am going to
assume the best." He opened another field dressing.

"You will be disappointed," Maris Solon said.

"In her? Perhaps."

"In her, but not in yourself," Wing said.

He was already disappointed in himself. He should have
discerned the pattern sooner. Should have taken Shi down the
instant he'd seen the sadist's face. *And then I would have been as
bad as the rest.*

There was no winning in the face of uncertainty. Act too
soon and risk slaughtering an innocent. Act too late and risk
allowing the slaughter of innocents. There was no good option
once slaughter was on the dance card. The only way to win was
to call the tune, and never let the fiddler bow the first note. Of
course, it would have helped if he'd recognized earlier that he'd
been invited to the céilí.

*Note to self: If there's three or more in a compartment assume
you're at a céilí. Even if you can't hear the piper.*

Ciarán pressed the field dressing to the young first officer. It
angled toward his wrist, refusing to adhere to her. The other
pair slowly dropped away to writhe on the deck for an instant,
before beginning to inch toward him. They were attracted, not
to him, but to body heat and the pulsing rhythm of blood
through veins. He reached up and closed her eyes.

"What do we do with Shi?" Zhao said.

"Stuff him in the autodoc," Ciarán said. "While I decide
what match needs making."

"There is nothing to decide," Danny Swan said.

"It's not your call," Ciarán said. "It's why we use a match-maker. You have too much skin in the game to think clearly."

Maris Solon touched her ear. "Literally."

"You misunderstand me," Swan said. "The chain around his neck. Pull it free."

Ciarán did as asked. There were six pendant spires clipped to the chain.

He heard the blood pounding in his ears.

"He bragged to me," Swan said. "Said I was not the first. I thought he meant Huangxu Eng he'd punished."

Ciarán took a deep breath. "Punished for taking the Oath."

"And for wearing the spire. But that was not what he meant."

Ciarán felt the blood drain from his face. He made a sound that didn't feel like words in his throat.

"You recognize one," Swan said.

"I don't," Ciarán said. "I recognize two. Both from *Thinker's Dame*. Lakshmi Ellis and Roisín mac Manus."

"Mac Manus the Stationmaster's sister?" Swan said.

"The Trinity stationmaster's sister by marriage," Ciarán said. And the mother of Ciarán's best mate. Missing and presumed dead since they'd been kids. Presumed dead by everyone but Macer Gant, who'd never given up hope.

"Admiral Shi appears to be a very bad man," Ciarán said.

"Do you think?" Konstantine said.

"I do. Who is going to help me stuff him in the autodoc?"

18

In the end only the Huangxu Eng pilot agreed to help him.

"I've only known the Admiral for a short while," he explained.

Ciarán laughed at that, but it turned out the man was serious. He wasn't one of the Mighty Eighty-Eight, but a pilot-for-hire, one stranded on Peaceful Dawn Platform when a customer blackjacked him and boosted his ship. If all the Mighty Eighty-Eight's pilots hadn't come down with the creeping rot at once he might yet be stuck on the platform, living out a slow death on the spindle and scraping by on hose-out work. "When I scored this gig, I thought I'd caught a break. All I really caught was a fast death."

Ciarán wasn't sure what all that meant. He was certain, though, who the customer would turn out to be before he asked.

"Another visiting professor," the pilot said. "Hector Poole."

"Another?"

"It's a parade," the pilot said. "Expert after expert."

"Expert in what?"

"Peaceful Dawn is a water extraction platform. Ice mining. Very old, almost played out."

"And?"

"Rumor is they found something."

"Found what?"

"Something that isn't ice."

"Something they needed experts for."

"Not just experts. *League* experts. Ones worth smuggling in."

"So, some sort of machine," Ciarán said.

"That's the speculation," the pilot said. "It's obsolete thinking, if you ask me."

"Says the smuggler."

"Says the man that's seen behind the curtain. The Empire *wants* foreigners to believe we're all meat puppets and slave masters. Five hundred years ago, even a hundred years ago that was true. But it's not so anymore."

"What's changed?"

"We got knocked up. The whole empire. Now we're carrying this mongrel baby and we're about to give birth."

"And then what?"

"I don't know. But whatever pops out won't bear the emperor's mug."

"Whose then?"

"The milkman's, most likely."

"Or the Dustman's."

"You said it, I didn't." The pilot scratched his chin. "I'll get his feet."

19

C iarán slipped into the first officer's seat and belted in beside the Huangxu Eng pilot. The cockpit was more like that of a longboat than a League shuttle. He recognized nearly every control. "Konstantine said she pegged the boards."

"Somebody did." The pilot ran his hands over the controls to no effect.

"What precisely does that mean?"

"It means the current flight plan is locked in and can't be changed."

"That doesn't seem possible."

"It's a dead man switch for situations exactly like this. I warned those maniacs. It's never been done. A handful of people stealing a League vessel intact."

"You told the Mighty Eighty-Eight it's never been done."

"Yeah, well, they weren't so mighty and there were only three of them left at the time. I figured abject and total defeat followed by ten days of shivering and starving on a Prescott Grange moon would have beaten some sense into them. But when they managed to steal an inspection team's shuttle it re-inflated their egos. And with the Admiral goading them on there was no talking sense."

"You couldn't turn yourselves in to the local authorities."

"Oh, I would have if they'd let me anywhere near the comms. But the Admiral is a frigging war criminal, and a bosom buddy of the emperor. Wing, too, would have been a prize. If they'd caught her, she would have hanged."

"For what?"

"Something she didn't do."

"According to Wing."

"According to her, sure. But the professor showed me proof. She wasn't around when the deed was done. Not that anyone will believe me, or her."

"The professor?"

"I told you. The Leagueman. Hector Poole. The joker who jacked my ride."

"Hector Poole stole your shuttle."

"What shuttle? He stole my *superluminal*. You think I'm some rock-hopper jock, and I smuggled him in *locally*?"

"I did," Ciarán admitted. "He stole your superluminal and he told you about Wing."

"While he was tying me up. He said the Eighty-Eight would need a pilot and that I should tell Wing he sent me."

"Wing, not Fang."

"Fang and Zhao both, they're like solid rocket boosters. Wing is the *igniter*."

"And the senior officer."

"Senior *surviving* officer. Your lady friend cut close to the bone there, earlier, with that crack about women and children first."

"I can see that. So Hector Poole ties you up. And he tells you to talk to Wing."

"Right."

"And then what?"

"And then he asked me if I had any questions, and I said sure, I gotta know, what did they find out there, that they were flying in all these experts for."

"What did he say?"

"Nothing, because I didn't really ask him that. It only occurred to me later. At the time I was busy disparaging his mother and threatening to hurt him next time I saw him." The pilot touched a control on the piloting board. Nothing happened. "Pegged down solid." He tapped his sleeve and a tiny pocket opened. He pulled out a joy stick. "I quit years ago, but the craving never really goes away." He touched the butt of the stick to the piloting console. "Been saving this for my last birthday."

"Keep saving it." Ciarán finished his survey of the cockpit. He recognized every control. There existed no secret League technology hidden amongst the controls. This was a bog standard, third-epoch League superluminal. That meant its drive worked exactly like every other Templeman drive. "I think I can get us out of this."

The pilot leaned forward in his seat. He pocketed the joy stick. "Do tell."

"You're not going to like it."

"I already don't like it."

"Wing will hate it."

"Then don't tell her."

"Good idea." Ciarán stood. "Let's go."

"You're going to tell *me*, right?"

"I will," Ciarán said.

"You *frigging* milkmen," the pilot muttered. "A simple yes or no would do."

20

T he plan was extraordinarily simple, but it depended upon several variables and impeccable timing.

Ciarán swung into the seat next to Helen Konstantine. He belted in.

Ciarán motioned for Maris Solon to join them. She inspected the drop module's control panel to Ciarán's left before adjusting the temperature and belting in beside him.

He tapped Konstantine's thigh. "I need to ask you some questions."

"Go ahead, Karen."

"I will."

"Why do you smile like that?" Solon said.

"Like what?"

"When she says your name. You smile."

"It's a hard name to pronounce."

"How do you say it?"

"Ciarán."

"KEER-awn."

"That's right."

"That's what I said," Konstantine whispered.

"It is, Pilot, no doubt. Now earlier, Maris Solon said something about *fleet* doctrine."

"Right. That's why I pegged the boards."

"The rest of that, breaching the tripwire at full boost, firing the drop modules at the station, is that also fleet doctrine?"

"It's doctrine to keep the ship from falling into enemy hands by any means available."

"But the means are entirely up to the officer in charge."

"Right. But we're an unarmed vessel without marines on board. The rest of the crew had already been rounded up. There weren't a lot of options."

"You could have jettisoned the superluminal drive."

"Not without dropping us into normal space first, where they might have allies waiting."

"They'd have to have allies waiting everywhere."

"If they witness our translation they can derive our route," Maris Solon said. "Then they need only deploy beacons along our route and a vessel to follow us."

"If they know our destination," Konstantine said, "All they really need is an accurate timestamp on our translation. The beacons are already out there on strategic routes like this."

"True," Solon said. "So long as they have the performance specifications of the hull."

Ciarán thought they were glossing over the hard part. "How do they read a normal-space beacon from Templeman space?"

"They do a dipper," Konstantine said.

"Periodically drop into normal space," Solon said. "Unless they are incompetent they would find us."

"Right. And once the drive is ejected we'd be easy prey," Konstantine said. "So long as they found us before we starved to death they'd have the hull, and they'd have us."

"And overloading the drive?"

Konstantine grinned. "It's what I'd have done, if there were witnesses. It's fast and final. But a vessel like ours, alone, with civilian passengers on board?"

"We'd be reported as overdue, and eventually listed as missing," Solon said.

Konstantine nodded. "Families need closure. It's not fleet doctrine. More like wardroom wisdom."

"But fleet doctrine is to overload the drive immediately," Ciarán said.

Konstantine shook her head. "No. I already said. That's what's taught at the Academy but it's not in the manual. The *manual* says it's up to the officer in charge to choose the means."

"The course and drop-in point at Sizemore. Is that set by fleet doctrine?"

"In a way," Konstantine said. "It's negotiated by traffic control officers based on fleet doctrine. As we're presently at war the parameters are tight. Normally it's a low velocity entry and a long walk to the station. The pilot confirms the parameters ahead of time."

"And the drop-in point is set prior to engaging the drive."

"It is that, just like on *Quite Possibly Alien*. The drive physics are different but the controls work the same."

"Then how did you alter our course and velocity to drop in at the tripwire under full thrust?"

"I didn't. I programmed a skip jump."

"Fast cycling the Templeman drive," Maris Solon said.

"It's how you do a dipper," Konstantine said. "That's what made me think of it."

"So we'll drop into normal space and then pop immediately back into Templeman space."

"Right," Konstantine said.

"How immediately?" Ciarán asked.

"It depends upon the drive," Maris Solon said. "Certain

vessels are designed for rapid response. Destroyers, courier vessels, other specialty hulls designed for search and rescue or pursuit."

"But not troop transports."

"By the second dip you'd be scraping the vomit off the deckhead," Konstantine said.

"Lovely image," Maris Solon said. "But I agree. A slow cycle. The design specifications will be noted in the ship's log."

"Best guess?"

"Ten seconds," Solon said.

Konstantine wobbled her head no. "I'd say fifteen, if it doesn't crack the bottle. This drive is *beat*." She grinned. "Either way, our families will have closure."

"That's grand," Ciarán said. "How long does it take to launch the life pods?"

"More than fifteen seconds," Konstantine said.

"You misunderstand," Ciarán said. "I mean, how long does it take from the time you push the button until the time they're making maximum thrust?"

Konstantine chuckled. "What difference does that make?"

"Well, I assume they have a limited supply of atmosphere. Running out a second too soon is no different than running out an hour too soon."

"But we don't have time to launch the pods."

"We can launch them in superluminal space," Maris Solon said.

"Agreed," Ciarán said. "You gave me the idea, with the talk about the drop modules. For that matter we could forego the life pods and just separate from the vessel in this module."

"Pods are better," Solon said. "They're engineered for survival and the launchers are designed to kick the pods clear of the Templeman drive radius, no operator required. The drop modules also lack rescue beacons."

"What about the pirates," Konstantine said.

"I'm going to go talk to them now," Ciarán whispered.

Wing's voice spoke from the compartment's control panel. "Save your strength. I can hear you clearly from there."

21

He crossed the compartment and knelt before Wing. It was an act of will, keeping his anger from rising to his face. She had his mother's death book open in her lap.

"I said I could hear you well."

"I like to look a lady in the eye when I make a proposal."

"Very well. I like it when men kneel before me."

Ciarán glanced at Fang and Zhao, crowding on either side of her. "Can you give us some air?"

"The compartment is filled with air," Zhao said.

"I am not so certain," Wing said. "Please verify that the furthest reaches of the compartment are fully stocked with air."

"I can see from here," Fang said. "All aired fine."

"Indeed," the pilot said. "Plenty of air. Speak, milkman."

The trio of Mighty Eighty-Eights seemed to notice the pilot for the first time.

"We will check for air," Zhao said. "The pilot will help us."

"But this was just getting interesting."

Fang unbelted and gripped the pilot by the collar. "Come with me."

"Does it bother you," Wing said. "When that one calls you names?"

"I *am* a tradesman. It's the life I've chosen."

"He calls you a servant."

"A mercenary servant. Not a slave."

"Your kind are everywhere."

"No doubt. Though the milkmaids outnumber the milkmen by a considerable amount."

"Is it true in general? There are still far more Freeman women than men? We thought this impression a statistical anomaly, or one based on historical bias."

"That there are more women merchants than men is absolutely true. It's a high-status occupation and ours a matriarchal society."

"Is your master a woman?"

"My employer, a merchant captain, is a woman. I'm presently acting as matchmaker for another woman, Captain Swan's sister. A ship's captain, like him. I don't have a master. At least not in the way you mean."

"Would you like one?"

"Would you?"

"Long term?" She smiled. "I think not. But for an evening? I might consider it. These women you serve. Do you love them?"

"There are many types of love."

"Are there? Have you seen them naked?"

"What?"

"The merchant. Have you seen her naked?"

"Of course not."

"The ship's captain?"

"I fail to see—"

"That is a yes. Your crimson face betrays you."

"I don't know where you're going with this."

"Would you like to see me naked?"

"I'm not opposed to the idea, but—"

"But what?"

"Not under the present circumstances."

"And why not?"

"I'm somewhat busy at the moment."

"We are sitting around waiting to die."

"There exists a way we might escape."

"I overheard your plans. There exists a way *you* might escape."

"How is this. There is a way you will live. And—"

"There are many types of living. What you propose is living long enough to be shackled. Living long enough to be paraded on a foreign dock. Living long enough to be murdered, and my death image flashed from screen to screen across the galaxy. To have foreign hands upon my corpse. Probing me. Dissecting me. Defiling me." Her dark eyes blazed. "That class of living is not to my taste. So I ask you again. Do you wish to see me naked?"

"I am not opposed to the idea."

"Very well." She reached for the crash harness latch.

He placed his hand on hers. Entwined his fingers with hers. "In a year. In two. In twenty. When you are happy and free. I would consider such an honor earned."

She struggled to pull her hand free. "Why do you *mock* me?"

He released her fingers. "Why won't you *listen* to me?"

"Because I've heard all you have to say."

He laughed out loud. "Now that would be a trick. Ask anyone."

"Leave me." She turned her gaze away.

"I intend to. But we should discuss my leaving first, so you'll know what I want you to do afterwards."

"What *you* want *me* to do?"

"I said that wrong." He gripped her chin and forced her to look him in the eye. "I don't just want you to do it. You *will* do it, else I'll hunt you down and murder you, afterwards. Does that class of living appeal to you?"

She glared black murder at him, outrage and hate beaming into his eye sockets, a plasma-beam of rage so distilled a single spark could ignite it.

Good. Now I've got your attention.

"No one has ever done this before," Ciarán said. "I don't think it has even been tried. And I doubt anyone could pull it off."

Her pupils dilated. She reached out, and grasped the neck of his utilities, and pulled his face close to hers.

"Go on," she hissed. "I'm listening."

"Shall I whisper the instructions into your ear?"

"Do it."

"Maybe we should agree on a safe word beforehand."

She pulled him closer. "Bite me."

"Good." That was a phrase, but he was fine with it if she was.

22

C iarán grunted as the escape pod launcher kicked. He glanced at Maris Solon, whose passive expression warred with the storm clouds behind her eyes. It felt like they were still accelerating but that couldn't be. The Templeman bubble was only slightly larger than the hull. He started to ask her about the physics of that feeling, just to keep her from repeating the same few phrases over and over again.

She beat him to the punch. "What sort of person robs another, knowing they're going to be picked up by the authorities minutes later?"

Maris Solon remained angry because Wing had removed Solon's bags of uncut gems from *this* escape pod and put them in *her* escape pod.

Ciarán decided it was safe enough to unbelt, so he did, and hand-over-handed it to the escape pod's tiny viewport. It was large enough for two to gaze out if they didn't mind bumping heads. The crown of Solon's head collided with Ciarán's chin. If Konstantine was right the ship's Templeman drive should disengage right about—

"Mark," Maris Solon said. She had a very nice handheld

and an antique wrist chronometer that looked quite expensive. She wasn't complaining that Wing had forgotten to steal those. "It's not translating."

"Looks that way," Ciarán said.

Something in his voice must have betrayed him.

"What did you do?"

"Me? I didn't do anything."

"You were talking with that strumpet for hours. Did you—"

"You'll note she's robbed me, too."

This was about the tenth time they'd discussed the theft of her gems and Ciarán's death book. That Wing had returned his mercenary company roster had surprised him. She'd demanded both books for her part in the operation.

"The vessel is not translating," Solon said.

And then it was. Suddenly they weren't hovering in a featureless void of black but moving rapidly across a field of bright stars. He couldn't locate Sizemore amongst the distant sparks but it was out there. And someone would notice their distress beacons.

Maris Solon held her chronometer in front of her face and performed a countdown. Ciarán noticed that she hadn't counted down from Konstantine's estimate of fifteen seconds but from her own of ten.

"Plus one, plus two," Ciarán solemnly intoned.

"Fine, so I was off by a few seconds."

Ciarán stopped counting at ten.

"Would we be safe if the drive let go right now?" Ciarán asked.

"We're still too close." Solon settled into her seat. "We'd fry." She belted in, seemingly out of habit. "So that's what you did. Engineered a drive failure. You imbecile."

"I had to at least try to save her."

"Your slutty mercenary."

"Konstantine." *Quite Possibly Alien*'s pilot had pressed a data crystal meant for Aoife nic Cartaí into his palm and motioned him toward the escape pod. They hadn't discussed who would stay behind to launch the pods when they'd discovered the automatic system had been sabotaged. It was her ship. That made it her duty. Helen Konstantine was iron when she'd made her mind up about something. And she'd made her mind up about this. He'd made up his mind too.

Maris Solon roared. "That wasn't your call, mister!" Her nostrils flared. "It's her command. Her duty. Her *honor*."

"I don't care about your navy rules or anyone else's. The first kind word I ever heard from a Leagueman I heard from Helen Konstantine. The first spacer to ever treat me like a man, and an equal? Helen Konstantine. On Ambidex Station, where I might have died in chains, the first voice to speak up for me? Helen Konstantine. So spare me the honor lecture. I'm trying to count."

"Count seconds."

"Escape pods. If there's four we're golden."

Maris Solon thumbed on her handheld. "There are three."

"Well. I thought I was done with the killing. Now I've got to chase down some maniacal Eng princess."

"Pirate queen, you mean."

"I mean what I say. Those in line for the throne have a look."

A look and a feel. When she'd pulled Ciarán close he'd felt the slight rise between her shoulder blades, the stiffening muscles of her upper spine. Like Agnes Swan, she would one day grow wings.

"Princess or not, I don't imagine any of us will be chasing down anyone. When that drive lets go—"

"It won't let go."

"I suppose you're an expert on Templeman drive failures. In addition to fixing tractors."

"I've read up on Templeman Drive failures."

"Have you? And when was that? During your lunch break at the grain elevator canteen?"

"Shortly after surviving a Templeman drive failure."

The troop transport remained stationary in relation to them.

"Here's an idea," Ciarán said. "Can your handheld detect life signs in the pods?"

"Three life signs in one pod," Solon said.

"That will be Shi, Captain Swan and the Huangxu Eng pilot."

"Or the hijackers."

"We'll see."

"And one life sign in the other."

Ciarán let out a deep breath. "Konstantine."

"Or a hijacker."

"It's Konstantine. The missing pod is the one we put the dead into. The Mighty Eighty-Eight didn't launch it."

The troop transport disappeared. Ciarán settled into his seat. Belted in. "They've jumped."

"Jumped?"

"Translated, I mean to say."

"They can't have. The controls are pegged."

"A drive overload takes priority. A bunch of processes that ordinarily run in the secondary core get promoted to the primary. And a bunch of processes that normally run in the primary core don't get shut down. But they do get shunted to the secondary core."

"Which processes?"

"I don't know. *The Bonehead's Guide to Starship Operations* wasn't specific."

"You're insane."

"Maybe. But I figure the details didn't matter, because you'd want the piloting controls unlocked during a drive containment emergency. Like if you were lashed to the station and the drive started to resonate. Or you were maneuvering in close formation and the bottle began to crack.

"But just in case that wasn't true I suggested the Mighty Eighty-Eights might want to slag the secondary core just as the drive overload began. It would take both luck and genius to get the timing right while clearing the fault." *And that idea made it irresistible.*

"The secondary core is responsible for life support."

"Is it? Well, let's hope Wing and Company had the sense to jump somewhere nearby."

"Jump somewhere nearby with my life savings," Maris Solon said.

"And with my mother's death book."

Maris Solon's handheld chirped. "We're being pinged."

Ciarán unbelted. "Who by?" He moved to the viewport.

"No transponder."

"Come here," Ciarán said. "I need a brain check." There was a ship out there. At least there was a ship's guts out there, not sprayed across the sky but neatly arranged, as if there were yet a hull around them. But there wasn't.

"I'm not coming there. Describe it."

"The innards of a vessel."

"That's *Lookdown*. They must have been expecting us."

"Who are they?"

"Aster's Army."

"What is it?"

"What it looks like. A vessel without a traditional hull."

"Weird."

"Experimental. The inner hull is a force plate. Think impact shielding meets containment field. The outer hull is a tunable filter set designed to obscure the force plate and its contents under various conditions.

"I can see the interior bulkheads."

"That's why it's best to ask for an inside cabin."

Ciarán's handheld pinged. It shouldn't have, because it was the one he purchased on Prescott Grange using his League work permit as identification. The device's id addy wasn't private, but he hadn't given anyone the code.

Ciarán glanced at the display. It looked like a text message but it read like a help message.

He turned the handheld upside down.

The message inverted.

He turned the handheld right-side up.

The message inverted.

"What are you doing?" Maris Solon said.

"It says rotate one-eighty."

Solon manipulated the tiny escape pod's control panel.

"Brace, brace, brace," she drawled.

Ciarán braced as she rotated the little pod on its axis.

Once the motion had stabilized he peered outside.

The handheld pinged again. "Huh."

Your chariot awaits.

That wasn't the sort of message anyone sensible would send a Freeman.

He passed the handheld to Maris Solon. "It's for you."

She shoved him out the way, monopolizing the viewport.

"What do they call that lump?"

"*Durable,*" Solon said.

"It doesn't look it." It looked like rubbish that had been resurrected from the family scrap heap that morning. Like there was still seagull crap plastering the windscreen.

"Belt in," Solon said.

"I say we stay here and wait for the see-through ship to rescue us."

"My deck, my rules."

"How did it become your deck?"

"You let me sit at the controls."

"You elbowed me out of the way."

"And you let your girlfriend steal my life savings. So we're even."

"She's not my girlfriend. I just met her."

The little pod's thrusters fired.

"That's a pity. If she *was* your girlfriend you'd know where she was headed."

"I know where she's headed."

"Because she confided in her prince."

"Because it's obvious."

"Good. Then you're coming with me."

"It's pretty obvious that I am. I'm trapped in an escape pod with you."

"Not for long."

The pod clanged against an airlock. Latched.

"I'm going through that airlock. You can stay here if you like. But you're welcome on board, so long as we have an understanding."

"Your deck."

"And?"

"Your rules."

"Good boy. Are you sticking?"

"How much reaction mass remains?"

"For the pod thrusters? We're dry."

"Can I see for myself?"

"She stole my life savings. And you *enabled* her."

"I don't see it that way."

"Don't you want your book back?"

"I want it back. But I haven't decided yet which I want more. That book or a future."

"Make your mind up."

"Is this *Durable* a fast ship?"

"No."

"Is Unity system on the way to Persephone?"

"No."

"I see."

"Is that where she's going? Persephone?"

"It is. Is Persephone nearby?"

"Yes."

"How near?"

"Two days. They'll have plenty of life support to make it. We won't be boarding a plague ship."

"That's not my concern." He'd miss the Merchant Guild examination. He wouldn't be getting promoted. And they might be so angry he'd disrespected them that they'd yank his apprentice license and kick him down Trinity system's gravity well.

So far he'd had a reasonable excuse, that he'd been hijacked. The Merchant Guild didn't accept excuses, but they might accept that one.

What they wouldn't accept is a *decision* he made, to hare off with the wealthy League captain who'd ignited a war with the Federation, all so she could recover her personal jewelry.

And they certainly wouldn't understand him blowing them off to recover a picture book his mother had made, one written in a language only he and a two-thousand-year-old starship could read, risking life and limb and raising the Guild's ire so he could read the book a third time and then burn it. Burn it to ash in less than a year.

And least of all, would they like to hear that he'd decided they could hang fire because he was worried that he might have *used* the Huangxu emperor's daughter, or niece, or cousin, used her mercilessly, and he needed to know that she was yet breathing, or forever give up the idea of being a man worthy of respect.

In desperation to save a friend he'd thrown away everything his mother had tried to teach him, thrown it all away without even noticing, because he still, somewhere beneath his skin, considered his people aggrieved, himself aggrieved, over something *Wing's* ancestors did to *his* ancestors. Wing was, in his hidden heart, *almost* as human as he and his friends. *Almost* as valuable.

He'd spit on Agnes Swan and the friendship growing between them. He'd spit on Old, and the Spear Bearers, on all those Huangxu who trusted him, trusted that when he gazed upon them, and told them that they were free men, and equals, he spoke, not just an objective truth, but the truth *inside* him. The truth in his head, *and* in his heart.

That he hadn't noticed his failure until it was too late only made it worse.

He hadn't found another way to save both Konstantine and Wing because he hadn't *looked* for one.

All his life he'd wanted nothing more than a merchant's ring. He wondered how it would feel on the finger of a man he despised.

"You were a great warrior," Ciarán said. "A senior captain?"

"I was that," Maris Solon said. "I still am."

"Then why were there no ribbons in your luggage? No medals amongst your jewelry?"

"Why do you think?"

"You don't need them anymore."

"That's the short story."

"And the long story?"

"I never needed them. I only thought I did. Now make your mind up. Stick or jet."

"May I use the comms?"

"If they work, you're welcome to use them."

"Stick," Ciarán said.

23

The tiny starship felt as small inside as it looked from the outside. It was three, perhaps four times the size of a longboat, but most of that space was taken up with engineering hardware. Ciarán managed to bang his head twice just getting out of the escape pod and setting the pod adrift. Not only did he have a headache but the second time his forehead hammered into a cross frame it drew blood. Freemen merchants were encouraged to remain current on their tetanus boosters, and now he knew why.

Moisture inside a hull was always a problem even on hulls in active service. But *Durable* was literally dripping, and so condensation-stained from years of disuse that it looked as if the hull had been submerged.

The docking hatch opened onto a tiny boat bay barely large enough to house a single planetary occupation shuttle, one so wedged in that it would take an ace pilot just to ease in past the snaking runs of exposed piping and conduits, also dripping and mossy backed, or so they seemed, though on close inspection it appeared to be not moss, but a thin layer of slippery green algae. At least the stuff wasn't growing on the deck or the deckhead.

A drop of ice-cold water landed on his neck as he shoved a loose wiring harness aside and followed Maris Solon forward to a narrow catwalk that bent around the bulging sphere of the Templeman drive, a catwalk so narrow that he had to walk it sideways, shoulder blades brushing the inner hull, his chest pressed tight against the drive containment sphere.

The catwalk led to a berthing compartment, very tight, stacked bunks, dormitory style, eight in all, four on either side of a narrow corridor. He glanced behind and noticed that his utilities had wiped a clean spot on the containment sphere, a sphere that he'd taken to be painted gray like the troop transport hull, but which was more likely to prove ivory or white hidden beneath a blanketing layer of grime.

Forward of the berths were a pair of ladders, one leading up, one leading down, and another skinny corridor between, a cramped refresher flanking the short walkway to port and a compact galley to starboard. Forward of that wasn't a hatch but a grimy walkthrough curtain, consisting of deck to deckhead strips of algae-coated transparent panels that shoved aside as Maris Solon continued her brisk walk. She stopped so suddenly that Ciarán stepped on her foot.

"Back off," she said, and he did, as much as he could. He was glad she hadn't asked him to turn around because he couldn't have, not without shoving her up onto the piloting console of the minuscule command deck.

Maris Solon dropped into the pilot's seat and pointed to the seat to starboard of her. "Park it."

Ciarán eyeballed the seat. It wasn't entirely caked with grime, but only because the mildewed cushions had split and whatever the stuffing was made of appeared toxic to all life. He sat and began to belt in. The crash harness latching hub came off in his hand as the dry-rotted webbing parted.

"I've felt cleaner after mucking out a bogside ditch." Ciarán wasn't certain what to do with the loose harness fastener. He couldn't leave it lying about for fear it would turn into a projectile. And he couldn't find the rubbish bin because he was riding in it. "How can you have clinging algae and dry rot in the same general vicinity?"

"Preflight," Solon said.

Ciarán glanced around the cockpit. He studied the controls in front of him. They were a mirror image of the controls in front of Maris Solon, with the addition of a sidecar of communications kit to his right. The controls didn't look any different than those of a League planetary occupation shuttle and he had a fair grasp of how those worked, thanks to Konstantine and Erik Hess. Overhead forward housed the toggles for the exterior inspection sensors. He powered the console up, surprised that it lit, and began flipping through the mechanical toggles that enabled and disabled the sensors.

He enabled the tomographic surveyor. While he waited for the system to begin the hull integrity scan he familiarized himself with the communications console. That seemed standard as well.

Solon pointed at the inspector display. "Kick the can scan to virtual and cycle the oglers."

She meant transfer the tomographic surveyor to an expert system and proceed to the visual inspection. Like priests and doctors, pilots had a different word for everything, not because they were needed, but simply to confound the layman.

"I'd like to watch it run." There were certain failure modes a human could catch that might go undetected otherwise. Given the state of everything else on the vessel he imagined the hull to be rotten through, or if not that, then a thruster mounting bracket or thirty, that would let go and send them spiraling out of control. He'd rather know about every life-threatening issue now rather than under boost.

"My deck—"

"Your rules. I know." He did as ordered, flicking through the exterior optical feeds. "There's mud caked on the belly plates."

"That happens when you crash land in a lake."

"Boosting back up through the atmosphere would surely burn that off."

"*Durable* isn't designed for atmospheric operation. They crated her up and towed her here." She pointed at the optical sensor display. "You can see where the lifting harness abraded the outer hull."

He couldn't see that, since he couldn't tell what had caused the hundreds of abrasions and dents that peppered the part of the hull he could see. "If it's not rated for atmosphere what was it doing landing in a lake?"

"Crash landing in a lake. And not designed for and not rated for are two different standards."

"So the vessel is atmosphere rated."

She laughed. "Work faster."

He watched her hands work. There was an economy of motion to her actions that came only with experience. She ran through a mental checklist with the steady motion of a machine. Seamus could likely preflight a vessel faster but only just. She didn't seem to be hurrying, but the work was getting done. She reminded him of his father, cutting and footing turf. Never sweating and never stopping, an all-day pace that would break a boy, no matter how strong and mighty. Professional didn't begin to describe it. Whatever there was beyond professional, where knowledge, and practice, and care turned mundane work into an offering and communion.

He flicked to the portside boat bay view and blinked. "You watched me cast the escape pod adrift, right?"

"Yes. Why?"

"Because it's back."

There was a pod attached to the boat bay hatch.

"That's not our pod."

Ciarán stood, pivoted on his heel, aiming sternward. He reached for the cockpit curtain.

A shoulder came through, followed by an arm, followed by the rest of her. Konstantine.

He smiled until he saw her eyes and the black thunder there, then the blur of a fist and a cloud of starry explosions behind his own eyes. He shook his head as his knees hammered the deck. A second fist. A knot of pain. His forehead struck the deck with a crack.

24

Ciarán's family kept donkeys. You can't keep donkeys and boys on a farm without a boy getting kicked, even if boredom was the cause, either boredom of the boy or boredom of the jack.

He had a vague recollection of what had hammered him across the jaw. Twice. And while it felt like a donkey's kick, complete with jarred teeth and aching bones, he was almost certain it was one of the two women he could hear talking. He was pitched up on a cot, and it didn't feel like his cot from home, because it wasn't a familiar cot. He cracked an eye open for an instant and the light felt like an icepick to the brain. On the second try, he opened them, and thought he should survey the damage.

In a minute he'd get up.

In a minute, he would.

bird pecked on his forehead. It pecked again.

When he opened his eyes, the pecking stopped.

"You wanted to use the comms," Maris Solon whispered.

He blinked, and sat up, and hammered his head into the bottom of the bunk above him.

"Hold it down, unless you want a tongue lashing."

"From you?"

"From your damsel in distress."

"So long as she doesn't pummel me again."

"We're outbound and less than an hour from translation."

He scrubbed his palm across his face. "Okay."

"If you want the superluminal node, you'll need to grab it now."

"I do want it. Can I afford it?"

"Its traditional for Lord Aster to provide free use of the node to those he's... interested in."

"Why?"

"So he can listen in."

"Right." Ciarán rubbed his forehead. "I should have known that. I'm really out of it."

"Then perhaps you should wait until we arrive in Persephone."

"I'd like that." Ciarán levered himself out of the bunk. "But this can't wait."

26

C iarán dropped into the first officer's seat. The seat cushion was yet warm, and the comms set already hot. Someone had been making or receiving calls, Maris Solon or Konstantine.

He scanned the comms log.

Erased. *That figures.* He'd intended to do the same after he was finished.

He *did not* want to make these calls.

He knew Lorelei Ellis's id addy by heart, and Macer Gant's. He rang them, one after the other. Both were unavailable, Lorelei's handheld shunting him directly to record mode, Macer's device not even reachable. He couldn't imagine leaving a message for Lorelei. *Your mother isn't missing anymore.* While Lakshmi Ellis wasn't Lorelei's birth mother, she'd been the only mother Laura had ever known. Laura had resigned herself that the *Thinker's Dame* had been lost with all hands ages ago. It was Macer who would be gutted, who hadn't ever given up hope that the vessel would return, and his own mother along with it.

Ciarán had to tell someone.

It only took one try to reach the Trinity Station stationmaster's office. It took twenty minutes to convince someone to loop the stationmaster into the circuit.

"What is it?"

"Lucan mac Tír?"

"Who else would it be? Is there another Trinity station-master I don't know about?"

"There isn't that I know of, sir."

"Good. Now speak or go off."

"It's better if we go visible spectrum."

"On your pingin?"

"If you like, sir."

"I like that better than me paying."

Lucan mac Tír was the oldest looking human being Ciarán had ever seen. His appearance wasn't a surprise, since everyone on Trinity Station knew the stationmaster's deck-striding gait and mane of white hair on sight. Ciarán had never looked the stationmaster in the eye, though, and even through the super-luminal node the impression was unmistakable. It was as if mac Tír had peered into the deepness of space and invited that vast emptiness to set up shop behind his eyes.

Ciarán aimed the comm station optics at the work surface and the chain of pendant spires he'd fanned across the narrow shelf.

"Do you recognize these, sir?"

"Of course I recognize a brace of pendant spires, you half-merchant whelp. I'm not senile."

"I'm glad to hear it, sir. What I mean to say is do you recog-nize these particular pendant spires?"

"You're glad, are you?" He squinted into his own optical feed. "Focus on them one at a time. Your sensor's rubbish."

Ciarán didn't think it was the sensor that needed adjusting but there wasn't any point in insulting the man. He did as ordered.

"Ach," he said. "*Thinker's Dame*. That will break the lad's heart when you tell him."

"When I tell him, sir? Aren't you Macer Gant's uncle?"

"By marriage. And I'm not likely to see or hear from him any time soon. He's been banned from the system and on the run from the debt collectors."

"That can't be."

"It can, and it is. You know that big ship of Truxton's he stole?"

"The *Tractor Four-Squared*?"

"Did he steal any other big ships from Truxton?"

"Not that I know of, sir."

"Good. Because he's in enough trouble as it is. Truxton had a financing deal on that vessel, an exorbitant rate and a balloon payment due. When word got out about the theft the Trinity Station Merchant's Bank called the loan."

"And Truxton's insurance paid out," Ciarán said.

"It might have, if he had any. No one but Luther Gant would have insured a vessel sight unseen, and even if he had, not against interstellar theft. On paper that hull doesn't have a superluminal drive."

"That sounds like Truxton's problem, sir."

"It would have been if the big planetary lummox hadn't agreed to square things by *buying* the vessel from Truxton and with it, the lien against it."

"Macer did that?"

"Do you know any other big planetary lummoxes around here?"

"Not—"

"I'm done looking at the spires. Point the sensor at yourself."

"I will," Ciarán said.

"I thought I recognized the name. Any *other* big planetary

lummoxes besides your man and yourself, is what I should have said, *merchant apprentice.*"

"I can tell you where you can find—"

"Listen here, junior. Your man is in a world of hurt, the sort of hurt that has bankers scanning open communication records for the mere mention of his name, and for any hint of where they can find him. Debt collector is just another name for matchmaker, if you ask me, and while they might rough up a deadbeat, they'll put the hammer down on a *runner*, and I don't mean just a kneecapping."

"I am informed, stationmaster."

"Good for you. Now aren't you supposed to be on Unity Station, preparing for your merchant examination?"

"I—"

"There's a file here on you, mac Diarmuid, a thick one, and I was asked to forward it on not twelve hours ago. I didn't read it because I'm a busy man, but I'm going to read it now. When you get to Unity Station they'll be a man there, and he'll receive those earrings from you and the story that goes with them. If he likes the story he might just lose that file."

"Understood, sir."

"Good to hear it. You'll know the man when you see him. Make sure it is a good story, lad, and whatever you do?"

"Sir?"

"Don't be late. Mac Tír out."

27

When Ciarán returned to the bunk, Konstantine stood waiting for him. She glared at him and blocked his path.

"Do you know why I hit you?"

"You're angry with me."

"I expected more from you. I thought we were friends. Comrades. I thought we were on the same side."

"We are."

"No. There's only one side. Your side. What you want and damn the price to everyone else."

"I was not going to leave you to die on that vessel. To waste your life for nothing."

"So my wishes are nothing? That makes *me* a nothing."

"You're the opposite. You're important."

"As a fixture in your world. As a non-player character."

"If that were true I would have left you to die."

"You have no idea, do you? No awareness of what you've done."

"I know I should have told you my plan."

"You should have butted out!"

Konstantine poked her finger in his chest. "Listen. I'm not like you and all the others. I'm not smart, or clever, or rich, or young, or pretty, or even likable. I'm average. I have no delusions. I'm an average pilot. An average military officer. An average woman. I'm fine with that. I wasn't always, but I am now, because I learned something in the thirty years I've worn the uniform. It's average people like me that *get it done*.

"We're the bulk of humanity. Most everyone you will ever meet will be like me. Nothing I do will ever blow anyone away. And until today, nothing I did ever utterly disappointed anyone.

"I was two days away from mustering out, two days away from receiving a handshake and a 'good job spacer' from some senior officer who couldn't pick me out of a lineup, which is *how it's supposed to be* for people like me.

"Now I won't get that. I won't be court-martialed. But I *will* end up, not as the villain in some Academy case-study, but as the *incompetent loser* who let three juvenile Skinnies steal a League interstellar.

"I'm no longer average. I'm sub-par. I don't know what they'll say about me. I abandoned ship. I surrendered. I screwed up and didn't peg the boards. I should have cracked the bottle the instant it looked like they might take the vessel.

"I'm not that smart. I'm sure there's a hundred more things the academics can dream up that I could have done that I didn't do. But I can tell you the one thing they won't dream up, because it is so *fantastically unbelievable* that it wouldn't occur to anyone but someone who's seen it with their own eyes.

"That a man I liked and respected would erase my life's work out of self-interest. Would steal what honor I had earned simply to let a bunch of hijackers escape. All because he fancied a pirate skirt."

Ciarán swallowed. "Is that what you believe?"

"I don't believe it. I know it." Konstantine pinched her

thumb and index finger together. "Here's what I am now, what the sum of my career amounts to." She jerked her fingers apart with a throwing motion. "An object lesson in failure. The poster girl for what *not* to do."

She turned on her heel and stalked away.

28

Ciarán pressed his forehead against the cold metal of the top bunk rack. His head throbbed, his heart ached, and there was nothing to do but bear it. Konstantine was entirely off base about his motives but as to his thought process? She was spot on. He hadn't considered her desires at all

"Is she right?" Maris Solon said.

Ciarán shifted so that he could see the woman. "You heard that."

"Pretty hard not to."

"It didn't occur to me. I'm not from an... organization-oriented culture. We'll fight and die for our families if we have to, and for our neighbors. But the idea that we'd give our lives to live up to some artificial standard of organizational behavior? It's counter to what I believe.

"*However*, I know Konstantine well enough to know what she believes. And I didn't bother to consider the situation from her perspective."

Solon leaned against the bunk beside him. "You understand her perspective."

"I don't. But I've watched her. Thought about her. Discussed her with the merchant captain and the ship."

"The ship?"

"The ship's minder, to be precise."

"You've served together on a sentient vessel?"

"*Quite Possibly Alien.*"

"And what did you and the ship conclude?"

"That Konstantine doesn't have nerves of steel—but she does have a strong sense of duty, ample respect for the command structure, confidence in the ship's captain, and less imagination than most. All of that together makes her *seem* to have nerves of steel. And makes her an ideal pilot for a second-epoch survey vessel."

"It makes her an ideal spacer in any navy in the wider world. She's right, wars aren't won by brilliant commanders, but by vast numbers of people like her. Where she's wrong in blaming you is that she listened to wardroom wisdom. She should have scuttled the vessel the minute she lost control of the situation. And what the Academy will do is study the case. And amend fleet doctrine to close the loophole that you exploited. Ultimately the fault lies with the Academy, for not accurately assessing human nature and constraining it."

"If she'd done that, she would have murdered us all."

"And she would have prevented a League military vessel from falling under Huangxu Eng control."

"Don't you people ever surrender?"

"We do. After the boat's been shot out from under us. But an intact hull, with a working superluminal drive? Not hardly."

"Well, I think that's crazy, but I know Konstantine doesn't, so I should have roped her into the plan."

"Or you could have respected her wishes."

"Her wishes were to kill us all where our deaths would be witnessed. My wishes were for me and everyone else on board to keep living. So, since my wishes and hers are equally valuable, I should have figured out what she really wanted and found some way for her to get that, while I also got what I wanted. I've ruined our relationship out of blindness and laziness. I've got to find some way to fix it."

"You might apologize."

"That wouldn't work. She'd know I was pretending. What I need to do is help her get her ship back. And give her the opportunity for a do-over."

"Another chance to scuttle the ship."

"She isn't really interested in scuttling the ship. What she thinks she wants is to die a navy hero before her hitch is up."

"And you're going to help her do that."

"I'm not. Did you not listen to what she said? That she's not fine with being average?"

"I'm not certain she said that."

"And I'm certain you're mistaken. Given what I now know about you people, I'd say your average navy hero is a dead navy hero. The living ones are the exception. Helen Konstantine might not believe it about herself, but I'm convinced she has the potential to be truly exceptional."

"And you're going to prove it."

"I'm not." Ciarán grinned. "We are."

29

Ciarán thought he was destined to spend an uncomfortable shift jammed into a planetary occupation shuttle with Konstantine glaring daggers at him and Maris Solon studying him like he was some sort of new species, but he lucked out. The shuttle's cargo bay was stuffed with gear, including an exo and a hardsuit.

He glanced at Maris Solon. "Ask her if she's ever used an exo." Konstantine still wasn't speaking to him. She wouldn't even be in the same compartment with him if Ciarán hadn't opened all of *Durable*'s hatches and vented the hull to space. It stunk inside the hull, and in time he'd get used to it, but he didn't want to get used to inhaling mold spores and rotting algae methane, and whatever else was producing the wretched reek.

He knew what he was doing. Once he'd been accepted to the Merchant Academy Ciarán had still needed a job, and he still didn't know anything worth paying for on a space station. But when it became clear that he wasn't going to flunk out, and he wasn't going to give up, the Academy had offered him a scutwork job cleaning hardsuits, the sort of work they made rule-breakers like Macer Gant do as punishment. And once it became clear he didn't mind scut work, would show up on time, and put in a full shift, they gave him more and nastier scut work until, by his junior year, he was earning enough as a hose-out tech and janitor to cover his tuition. He knew how to clean a hull, and first thing you needed to do?

Kill everything in it. There was no faster or more thorough way than to power everything down but essentials, put those in standby, and let the vast, seeping coldness of space work its way into every hidden cavity and gunk-caked crevice. He might not get it all, there were viruses that could survive for a while, and they didn't have the refresher capacity to scrub themselves, all at once, but it was a start, and would cut down on the risk they'd catch something nasty. A risk Maris Solon discounted, and Konstantine hadn't even considered, so consumed by her rage at Ciarán.

"She's a Royal Navy spacer," Solon said. "She was born in an exo."

"Reborn," Konstantine said.

"Life begins at induction," Solon said. "It says so in the fine print, when you take the queen's shilling."

"Well, that explains my confusion," Konstantine said. "I hadn't learned to read back then."

"Truly?" Maris Solon said.

"It wasn't expected of us."

Ciarán didn't want Konstantine looking backward. He needed her facing forward.

"I don't know how to use an exo," Ciarán said. "So I'll take the hardsuit, if it comes to that."

"You didn't ask if I knew how to use one," Maris Solon said.

"I didn't, because your name is stenciled on this one," Ciarán said.

"And if we need three suits?"

"We can draw straws." Ciarán's handheld beeped. *Or someone can volunteer to be a hero.* "Time's up. Close the hatches and re-pressurize the hull."

"Close the hatch and re-pressurize the hull, please, Maris."

"Do I get to call you that? Maris?"

"It would help if you did." She pressed a glyph on her handheld. "I need to get used to it."

"Would you prefer I called you something else?"

"Senior Captain," Konstantine said. "Captain. Sir."

Ciarán grinned. "I was thinking something like 'Lady Solon', or 'Your Eminence'."

"It's 'Your Grace'," Konstantine said.

"Are we on speaking terms now, Pilot?" Ciarán cycled through the optical sensor feed displays on his handheld.

"I much preferred 'Captain'," Maris Solon said. "It felt like something I'd earned. The others feel..."

Ciarán thumbed to the security status display. "Pompous?"

"Like hand-me-downs. Not anything I would have chosen. Now I'm..."

"Adrift," Konstantine muttered.

"Maris." she said. "Simply Maris. I'll need to get used to that. To discover how it feels. What it means to be ordinary."

The hatches appeared closed. Ciarán nodded to himself. "That's a terrible plan. The hull?"

Maris Solon glanced at her handheld. "Pressure rising. And it isn't a *plan*."

"Tell me about it." Ciarán stood and picked up what passed for a janitor's mop on League starships. "That's what makes it so terrible."

"I suppose you have a better idea," Konstantine said.

"Not always. But in this case, I do."

"Let's hear it," Konstantine said.

"You're not really interested in hearing what I have to say. You're only interested in not hearing it, and putting words in my mouth, and then dismissing your own invention as rubbish."

"I'd like to hear it," Maris Solon said.

"Fine. I'll whisper it to you."

"Now you're being petty," Maris said.

"I'm not. I'm *discovering* how it *feels* to be Ciarán mac Diarmuid, with this crew, on this vessel."

Maris Solon stared at him.

Ciarán turned to face Konstantine. Looked her in the eye. "I understand, Pilot, that you're angry at me. And I accept that you're right to be. But you cannot read my mind, so you really have no idea why I did what I did. What my motives were. And I could try to explain myself to you. But I'm not going to. Anything you need to know about me you can learn by watching me.

"Give up your grudge. I'm not swayed by your approbation. I'm not accepting of your guilt. I'm not cheered by your affection or praise. I am as impervious to the opinions of others as glass, and as transparent. I am not the man you *imagine*.

"I failed you, and I regret that. I regret it because I am not yet the man I aspire to be."

"I thought you were a better man," Konstantine said.

"You thought I was a different man."

"An aspiration isn't a plan," Maris said. "It's a hope. A wish."

"It's less than that. It's the antonym of destiny."

"And if I aspire to be a woman of destiny?"

"Then you don't need a plan. And you don't need to work the plan."

Maris Solon stared at him.

Eventually she spoke.

"I'd rather drive than ride."

"The high and mighty have that choice. It's simpler for the rest of us."

"You'd rather drive than walk."

"We'd rather drive than crawl," Ciarán said. "Or kneel."

"I'd rather fly than drive," Konstantine said.

"Good," Ciarán said. "Because my plan depends upon your doing that."

30

C iarán leaned on the mop handle and surveyed his handiwork. There were several reasons he liked cleaning; not least of which, it was hard to make things worse, excepting for collectibles and such, and excepting if you used the wrong cleaner. Now that he thought about it, it was easy to make things worse if you didn't know what you were doing, but he did, at least in regard to cleaning farmsteads and starships.

Another thing he liked about cleaning, it kept him moving. And with the temperature dialed down in the hull he needed to *work* to stay warm. They'd be able to turn the heat up once he was done shearing off all the ice, which came off the formerly dripping pipes and surfaces in sheets thanks to a miracle chemical he'd found in the same storage locker with the mop, a thin liquid that freed the ice from whatever it was layered atop without appearing to damage the surface below. He had a dozen large bags of frozen algae and ice resting beside the boat bay airlock. They were heavy, and he would have spaced them already, if he hadn't grown up on a farm, where you rarely threw anything away without first thinking about how it might be repurposed first.

And that was the third thing he liked about cleaning. The work was interesting enough to fend off boredom, but not so demanding that he needed to remain focused on the job. He could work and think at the same time, and he wasn't going to break anything or kill them all if he let his thoughts wander. And wander they did. He had a lot to think about.

First there was the issue with Konstantine. It wasn't the most urgent issue, but it was the most important. He liked her. Liked her and admired her. Even though he wouldn't let it alter his actions, he liked it better when she and he were on good terms. He didn't think he liked her just because she was useful to him, but it was difficult to tell. He was on the hook for a lot now, not just merchant-apprentice work, but also keeping *Quite Possibly Alien*'s minder from scouring life from Freeman space, keeping ten mercenary companies he'd saddled himself with fed, not to mention winning a merchant license. Or, barring that, at least keeping his apprentice license alive so he wouldn't end up back on the farm, shoveling manure and mucking ditches.

He hadn't expected to find an exo on board, or a planetary occupation shuttle either. He hadn't expected to be on board a ship at all, but bobbing in an escape pod, watching the voltage on the rescue beacon batteries drop while praying for a salvation of someone else's making—an uncomfortable feeling, and one he'd prefer not to experience in its fullness.

Given the wealth of murderous resources now available to him, the problem became one of locating Wing and the troop transport. He was nearly certain that he'd rigged the situation so that Wing would go to Persephone. But nothing involving other people was a certainty, strangers and foreigners least of all. Assuming he could find the vessel, the rest would be child's play. Shuttle over, enter through any of the vacant drop module hatches, and board in an exo. The monstrous exoskeletal armor was unstoppable with any of the weapons Wing possessed. The Mighty Eighty-Eight would either have to surrender or die in a one-sided bloodbath. He didn't want a blood bath and would strive to avoid it, but if that was what it took to put Konstantine back in control of that vessel, and to send her jetting back to Sizemore it would happen. There was no Freeman rule that said you had to lie down and agree to be robbed, or to stand by and let your friends be robbed. Whether there would be a fight or not was entirely up to Wing. He liked her but he didn't owe her.

Konstantine was entirely wrong about his relationship with Wing. Wing was like those sacks of algae and ice by the hatch, dead weight maybe, likely to be jettisoned, but potentially useful to keep around if he could figure out a reason to do so. And unlike disposing of frozen waste, he had a moral duty to find some way to preserve her and the rest of the Mighty Eighty-Eight if he could, not for her sake, or theirs, but for his own.

He'd done a lot of soul searching after the dustup in Contract system, and decided that he'd grown too cavalier about life, his own and others'. He didn't have the right to declare anyone evil and end them. That was a given. But he also didn't have the right to step aside and allow others to do the same, even if he agreed that they were probably right.

He'd become a merchant because he believed the best way to build a better tomorrow was by helping others succeed. Peacefully collaborating, by divvying up the load and pulling together. That's how civilized people made progress.

He'd never imagined he get drawn into one kill-or-be-killed situation after another. And he'd never imagined he would have to take a life or decide who lived and who died. He wasn't haunted by what he'd done, not if he thought it through, but he'd been lucky. He hadn't made a soul-destroying mistake because the right and wrong of it seemed clear cut at the time, and remained so, upon reflection.

Wing and the Mighty Eighty-Eight were the first truly gray confrontation to entangle him. They were lawless, no doubt, and likely ruthless when they needed to be. But were they *evil*?

He wasn't sure. There weren't Freeman police. There were barely any Freeman *laws*. And the ones that existed were of recent vintage. Not everyone, Ciarán's dad included, believed that any law that had to be enforced with guns was legitimate. Ciarán wasn't used to thinking about right and wrong as anything but personal decisions. Any disputes and disagreements between parties were worked out by talking and arguing, and either agreeing or agreeing to disagree. If the perceived wrong in question seemed to demand a blood price, it became a matter for the matchmakers to work out, family agents, no third parties allowed. From the outside, it might seem like anarchy and prone to prolonged back and forth feuding, but in practice that rarely happened. When it did the neighbors got involved and put an end to it. There was a great body of lore built up around matchmaking, with the concept of balance taught in school and the administration of justice carried out daily over farmhouse tables and in family ship mess compartments across the Federation.

When Ciarán had flicked a sleepy dart into Admiral Shi's eye instead of a murder dart into his jugular vein it wasn't an act of vengeance, but of balance. An eye for an ear seemed a fair price for Danny Swan's mutilation, if not for his subsequent imprisonment and humiliation. Agnes Swan might not agree, but Ciarán knew from experience that those were money debts, not blood debts—on the island if not the station, and he was an island man. Thus the balance had to feel right by island standards, else he'd just be making up the rules as he went along.

He hadn't expected Shi would fall face-first, and jam the dart deeper into his eye, but that was down to the hand of prov-

idence and not to Ciarán's accounting. Ciarán wasn't unhappy
with the fact, but it hadn't entered into his weighing of the facts.

Nothing Wing and the Mighty Eighty-Eights had done to
him or his had risen to the level of a blood debt. What blood
was shed was between their own, and between Shi and the
League.

Admiral Shi was undoubtedly evil, had done evil against
the first officer he'd bang sticked and caused to die, an *unneces-*
sary and unprovoked use of force against a captive right in front
of his eyes. It wasn't as if Ciarán had heard about this after the
fact. He'd witnessed the woman's death.

Had Shi died at Ciarán's hands he wouldn't lose a minute of
sleep over it. Just like he no longer lost sleep over the Huangxu
Eng hijackers he'd accidentally killed on Ambidex station.

Wing and the Mighty Eighty-Eight were hijackers. Pirates.
He was fully in his rights to fight back against such persons,
including fighting to the death. But the two situations, Shi and
Wing, felt entirely different to him, though they might not feel
that way to Maris Solon, or Helen Konstantine. He'd been
robbed, and stunned, and embarrassed, but he'd not once felt
in danger for his life from Wing and the Mighty Eighty-Eight.

He couldn't very well go around murdering everyone in the
wider world who embarrassed him or tried to rob him. He had
to draw the line somewhere, and he'd drawn it to his own satis-
faction.

Killing would be a last resort when confronted by evil he
couldn't ignore.

Therefore, he needed to come up with some way for
Konstantine and Maris Solon to take back the ship while Wing
and her crew weren't on board. Which was made easier by the
fact that Wing was a royal, no matter how minor, and Fang and
Zhao her personal bodyguards. He should have noticed that
fact earlier, but it hadn't been clear at first. It was only later,

once Shi was out of the picture, and after he'd had time to think, that the relationship became apparent to him.

Given that, the easiest way to get them *all* off the vessel was to get *Wing* off the vessel.

Ciarán worked his way forward to the berthing compartment. He parked his mop and peeled out of his utilities. Caked with grime, he hoped the compact refresher could get his tractor mechanic's outfit clean enough that it didn't feel stiff when he moved his limbs. He pulled a blanket off a top bunk and draped it across his shoulders. It was bitter cold, and the blanket, like the bunk, sized for a smaller class of person.

The blanket proved useless against the cold, and the refresher proved slower than it ought, so he washed up in the micro-galley sink, toweled off with the pillowtowel from his bug-out bag, and climbed into the lower bunk shivering. He wasn't tired but frigid, so he found the data crystal Konstantine had handed him on the troop transport, the one with messages for Aoife nic Cartaí. He had time. It wasn't that he wanted to read the merchant captain's mail, but he needed to, in case there was some urgent message he might need to relay through Persephone's superluminal node. He doubted he'd have time to review the messages once in orbit.

Ciarán took a deep breath and began.

T here were a number of messages on the data crystal, not a single one of them addressed to Aoife nic Cartaí. The crystal appeared to contain an archive of messages and attached documents, all internal to the League War Department, all discussing Konstantine, Hess, and Amati, the three members of *Quite Possibly Alien*'s crew in the League military and on detached duty.

Three of the messages he'd already seen and passed on, messages ordering Konstantine, Hess, and Amati to present themselves and report in. There were two nearly identical sets of messages to the trio, one set reporting that they were being cashiered, and another set that indicated they'd been recalled to active duty. It wasn't until he examined an earlier series of messages, an internal War Department exchange, that the rest of the messages began to fit into place. This was an internal intelligence file. And the subject wasn't Konstantine, Hess, and Amati.

The subject was *Quite Possibly Alien*.

As he dug through the attachments the plot became clear. A heated argument raged from message to message, one centered around what to do about a sentient starship that was considered insane by the bulk of all synthetic intelligences surveyed, and not only insane, but dangerously so.

As it was difficult to act without full knowledge, those members of the crew subject to recall were ordered recalled purely as an excuse to chemically interrogate them regarding the vessel. A good decision demanded good data. Hess, Amati, Konstantine. They would begin with those three.

There was included a detailed transcript of Konstantine's interrogation, and a memo summarizing the results. The interrogation didn't appear to center upon Konstantine's assessment of the ship's sanity, or dangerousness, but rather focused on a detailed technical debrief regarding the ship's operations and the technology she'd observed. The report concluded that the technology was uniquely valuable, and that, while Konstantine could operate the vessel's controls, she had absolutely no idea how the mechanisms behind the controls worked.

Of the three Hess would prove the most valuable to debrief, but in their opinion, there were two additional members of the crew uniquely qualified to assist in their assessment; Maura Kavanagh, the ship's navigator, who possessed a unique understanding of the vessel's superluminal capabilities and navigational theory, and Ciarán mac Diarmuid, who, according to Konstantine, was the ship's ally and confidant.

There followed an extended discussion about how they might convince Kavanagh and mac Diarmuid to help with their research, followed by a discussion about how Maura and he might be abducted and interrogated, followed by a discussion about how such an abduction could start a war with the Freemen if it was discovered and traced back to them.

Their conclusion? Start the war with the Federation first over something trivial. *Then* abduct the spacers. Whatever happens to them then happens during the war. Capture them, interrogate them, execute them while trying to escape. Or simply disappear them. Capture the vessel and hand it over to the boffins for disassembly and analysis. Resolve the trivial matter, end the war, and move on.

Subsequent to that discussion was another discussion, one declaring that idea insane. The ship's technology couldn't be valuable enough to risk a war with the Federation. It would be simpler and more effective to simply find the vessel, follow it, and destroy it, preferably in Huangxu space. The vessel couldn't possibly be as dangerous as reported. A properly constituted task force could deal with every conceivable threat.

There followed a detailed risk assessment of which plan posed the least risk. The study concluded that both were equally risky.

A cost-benefit analysis was also attached. It concluded that the cost of each was equivalent, but that the benefit could be maximized by executing both plans in series. Attempt the abductions, capture the vessel, and reverse engineer its technology. If that didn't work, eliminate the vessel in secrecy so that its secrets couldn't fall into enemy hands.

It's already in enemy hands, one of the most strident responded.

The last document in the file was a scanned image of a handwritten note. One that appeared to be written on flash paper.

Do it. Steyr.

The refresher chimed.

Ciarán was climbing into his freshly laundered utilities when Konstantine and Maris Solon entered the compartment. He zipped up and studied their faces, searching for the lie. For the betrayer. He wasn't certain that he believed the story in that damning file. It was a little too perfectly documented. A little too complete and specific in every detail. But he couldn't shake the feeling. *What if I've already been abducted?*

Which was a crazy idea. There were too many ways any

abduction plot would have already been thwarted. Unless he was complicit in his own abduction, any conspiracy would have fallen apart already. Except the abduction might be yet to come, and it didn't matter where he ended up, so long as he was isolated and off the grid, and they knew where to find him. The comms log onboard had been wiped.

That wasn't all that unusual and wasn't in itself evidence of anything nefarious.

Konstantine was a given. They might be at odds, but they were on the same side.

He could decide to either trust Maris Solon or not.

Macer didn't trust her.

But Seamus did.

And now that he thought about it, there *was* someone he knew who compiled perfectly crafted and bloodless intelligence files. Someone who would send such a file to Aoife nic Cartaí. According to Seamus he'd made some deal with Aoife nic Cartaí's grandmother, and was now working for her, at least part time.

The more he thought about it the more certain he became.

Seamus had assembled that file.

Ciarán glanced at Maris Solon. "How long until we make Persephone?"

"Eight hours and change. Is something wrong?"

"I'm not sure. I need to use a superluminal node to be certain."

"Persephone has one," Maris said. "I checked."

"Did you?" Ciarán scratched his eyelid. "When was that?"

"Right after Hector rang off," Maris said. "While you were recovering from your..."

"Ass kicking," Konstantine said.

Maris chuckled. "Yes. From that."

"Hector is Hector Poole? The man Konstantine calls the Dapper LT?"

"The same."

He glanced at Konstantine. "And he gave you the data crystal you gave me?"

"That's right. Why?"

"Did you look at the contents?"

"I would have, but someone stole my handheld."

"When?"

"Later that day. I didn't have time to get a new one."

"So you haven't seen the contents."

"No. Why? Is it bad?"

"Maybe. When's the last time you were chemically interrogated?"

"When they recalled me to active duty."

"And what did they ask you about?"

"How would I know?"

"What do you mean?"

"I mean *how would I know*? I don't remember. What's this about?"

"How can you not remember? That's not so long ago."

"The drugs are designed to suppress memory," Maris said.

Ciarán found that unlikely. "The ones used on me didn't."

"It's a fleet requirement. The same questions are asked of thousands daily. The process is designed to make it harder to cheat. Harder to prepare a lie."

"You can lie under chemical interrogation?"

Maris Solon seemed reluctant to reply. "Some can."

"Huh." Ciarán hadn't imagined that possible. He glanced at Konstantine. "How well do you know this Hector Poole character?"

"I haven't seen him for years," Konstantine said. "Until the other day."

Ciarán turned to Maris Solon. "And you?"

"I know him as well as anyone does, I suppose. Which is to say, not at all."

"Do you trust him?"

"No," Konstantine said. "He's a self-serving snake."

"He's Lord Aster's fixer," Maris Solon said.

Ciarán watched Maris Solon's eyes. "I don't know what that means."

"It means he's a self-serving snake," Konstantine said.

"He is as trustworthy as any man who lies for a living."

"I see."

"You remind me of him," Maris Solon said. "Not physically of course, or how you speak. But how you think. How you never come straight at a topic. How you hide your cards and only reveal them after the hand is played. How you use people without them even noticing."

"That's a lot to know about someone in a short amount of time."

"It's my specialty. Studying people. Determining what makes them unique."

Konstantine laughed. "And then beating it out of them."

"Sometimes. If that's what's required to make them effective warriors." She looked Ciarán over. "If you and Hector ever met, I think you'd like each other very much."

"I have met him," Ciarán said. "Years ago. During what you people call the short war."

"Good heavens. You might have said." She shoved him aside. Glanced at the mess on his bunk. He'd emptied his bug-out bag, searching for the data crystal. "I thought that Huangxu hussy stole your books."

"Huangxu Eng. And I agreed to give the books to her," Ciarán said. "In exchange for her help rescuing Konstantine. It's how I knew she'd come here. There's a museum on Persephone that pays big money for death books."

"Who told you that?"

"Hector Poole did. Years ago. During the short war. It wasn't like we had a conversation about it. It was just—"

"Something he said in passing," Maris Solon said. "A throw-away line."

"Right."

She picked up the book from the bunk. Flipped through it. "It's in Huangxu."

"Huangxu Eng," Ciarán said. "The company commanders are educated men."

"These are mercenary companies."

"Now they are. They were elite troops in their day."

"And when was that?"

"For most of them? A thousand years ago."

"You're joking."

"I'm not. They were property. Put in cold storage once it was clear they were obsolete. A few would awaken now and then to inquire if they were needed, but mostly? They remained in cryo."

"Why do you have this book?"

"Because I'm an idiot. I thought to buy one company's freedom and I ended up responsible for ten."

"You're *responsible* for them?"

"I signed a contract to that effect. Right now they're in Contract system, helping the stationmaster clean up a mess there."

"There's a secret weapons lab in Contract system," Maris Solon said.

"Apparently it's not very secret," Ciarán said.

"Hector told me about it." She flipped the book closed. Gazed at the cover. Tapped it with her index finger. "What does this text say?"

"Roster, Tally, and Accounts. The company commanders are conservative and prefer to keep paper records as backups."

"Understood." She tapped again. "And this? What does it say?"

"The Legion of Heroes."

She gripped the bunk upright. "I need to sit down."

"Then do it in the cockpit," Ciarán said. "The both of you. And take this data crystal with you."

"What for?" Konstantine said.

"Plug it in. Review the contents. That way we'll all know what we've stepped in. Maybe together we can come up with some ideas."

"Ideas about what?" Konstantine said. "About how we scrape the mess off our shoes?"

"Perhaps." Maris Solon looked him in the eye. "Unless we've stepped in it up to our elbows. Have we, *Knight Commander*?"

"Probably not for the pilot, or yourself," Ciarán said, "but I'll be wanting a snorkel."

32

C iarán sat on the bunk and replayed the events since receiving the notice to appear before the Merchant Guild licensing board. The simultaneous recall of Aoife nic Cartaí to Trinity Station. The need to travel alone, without weapons, without Wisp, under a known alias—to Hector Poole at least—seemed designed to leave him vulnerable, isolated, and easy to abduct.

Suppose that were all true, that events were manipulated in such a manner, who would need to be in on it? A very few people, two, three, hidden amongst crowds. A clerk in the Guild, who set the date for Ciarán's examination to coincide with Aoife's recall to Trinity Station would be all it would take. All the rest might reasonably flow from that one action, once the war was on.

Maris Solon had started the war.

She didn't seem the sort to do that by accident. She was either in on the plot, a pawn, a useful idiot, or blackmailed, her loved ones threatened perhaps. Operating under duress seemed most likely given what Ciarán knew of her nature from observing her.

There might not even be a plot at all. It was too perfect, the details outlining a scenario that precisely matched his fears that *Quite Possibly Alien* was too valuable, too dangerous, too powerful, and too unpredictable for the League to allow it freedom in the wider world.

That the vessel was sentient and considered a citizen under League law could explain why the League hadn't moved to claim the vessel. But those were laws made by men through treaty, not guaranteed rights, and therefore subject to amendment.

The League clearly no longer feared war with the Federation, a reasonable belief, given what he knew. The Federation didn't want a war, any war. Forced into one they would find the most expedient excuse to end the conflict, not on principal, but upon interest. The League was the Federation's largest competitor, but they were also its largest trading partner.

It was well understood *Quite Possibly Alien* was considered mad. As a danger to purely itself it continued to possess all the rights of an adult. But as a danger to others? If the League declared the vessel incompetent and subject to removal and confinement? Who would argue with that as their income statements bled red by the hour? He could hear the excuses in his mind.

Had the vessel taken the Oath the case might be different.

Ciarán didn't think that *Quite Possibly Alien* was insane. He knew it. If it were sane, it would have destroyed the world the instant it had seen the shape of it: twisted as it was, one self-serving excuse wrapped around another, not a chain forged by despots as Freeman feared, but a rope, braided from cowardice and greed, one grown long and stout enough for a hanging.

That the noose draped from their own necks and the necks of their children seemed not to matter. It chaffed but it did not bind. Not yet. Not today. Not this hour.

Not this second.

Perhaps if he had been born without a birth defect he might understand. He had no sense of what it cost a man or a woman to be brave. To face an unknown future choked by fear. Clearly the price was high. He could read it on the faces of those around him. Of those he loved.

He was born a free man. He knew nothing of their struggle. So he tried to not judge others. There were too many people in the world, too many ways of living. Yet he found he couldn't help himself, in moments like this. Sorting. Sifting. Ranking.

Who was on his side?

Whom could he trust?

It didn't seem to matter; the language they spoke, the gods they worshiped, the uniform they wore, the shape of their limbs, the color of their skin, the source of their consciousness or the fuel that sustained them.

He knew an ally when he met one.

There was no oath one spoke, no pledge of fealty, no hidden sign or secret handshake. He hadn't understood all this when his world had ended at the shoreline. He'd misjudged *Quite Possibly Alien* and her crew, misjudged them terribly, because he'd not yet learned to look beneath the surface. A vessel wasn't defined by the shape of its hull. It was the engine that drove it that mattered.

He'd meant to use Wing, to trick her, or bend her to his will, whatever it took to save Helen Konstantine, and perhaps himself. He didn't owe Wing anything. She and her crew had violated the most fundamental of Freeman customs, the prohibition on the *unprovoked* use of force. He therefore had no obligation to respect her person or desires, and no intention to do so.

She had stood between him and a merchant's license. He had decided not to hate her because one didn't hate a bump in the road. One drove over it or swerved around. He had been angry, though, not simply because she had robbed him, but because she had *violated* him. His mother's death book had lain open on her lap.

There could be no swerving around, not after that. There would be a head-on collision whether she realized it or not. And once he got what he wanted, he would be done with her. He had gazed down upon her and felt nothing but sorrow.

Then she tapped her finger against his mother's death book and said—

33

"I know this story."

Ciarán nodded. "I doubt that."

"Doubt it all you want. It is the tale of the farmer and the willow wife."

"You can read a dead language. One written in cursive script."

"Why would I need to?" She patted the seat next to her. "This book has pictures."

"Not here." He motioned toward the far end of the compartment. "Over there."

"Excellent. Shall we get naked before we read? Or afterward?"

If she could truly read what his mother had written—he'd stand bare before her, whether he wished to or not.

"Afterward," he said.

"Excellent."

WING SAT with the book open in her lap. "Imagine my surprise at finding a picture book. And imagine my surprise at finding a story I knew in the pictures."

"I'm imagining that," Ciarán said.

"This is not a story from the Hundred Planets," Wing said. "It is much older, from the days before we were Eng. Yet it is still told, and worse, still argued over."

"Argued over?"

"Oh yes. Argued and fought over. At one time a man could be beheaded for telling this story." She winked at him. "Or for listening to it spoken."

"Why?"

"Hear it, and see if you can tell. Are you ready to begin?"

"I'm ready," Ciarán said.

"You don't look ready. Place your hand in mine, and rest your chin upon my shoulder."

He did as asked.

She stroked her thumb across the back of his hand. "Very good. Now see the picture, is it a boy or a man seated beneath the gracefully arching branches of the willow?"

"A boy."

"I think so, too. What shall we call him?"

"Junh," Ciarán said.

"We can't call him that. Junh will not be born for another two thousand years."

"You pick, then."

"He is called Min Sheng," she said. "He is a rice farmer. While he rests beneath the willow he dreams. Do you know what he dreams of?"

Ciarán tapped his head against hers. "Tell me."

He could not see her smile but he felt it when she did.

34

Min Sheng often dreamed of the night sky, and of the stars. The world in flux, Min Sheng clung tight to those distant companions, who hid by daylight, contested monthly with the moon, and danced on these nights when they ruled the heavens alone.

Like his neighbors, Min Sheng lived in a small village beside a great, sluggish river. There, in the shadow of a snow-capped peak, the heavens remained perpetually clear at night, though they often clouded and showered in the afternoons. Then Min would race for the shelter of the ancient willow, its branches shedding sunlit droplets at the stirring of the slightest breeze, scattering bright jewels and whispering to him, as the stars often did.

He would rest his back against the tree's strong trunk and watch the rain fall and the river swell, its surface rain-pocked pewter beneath the clouds, tirelessly sweeping past beneath draping branches. The river did not speak to Min, its current deep and silent with nothing worth saying to a boy. Perhaps when he grew older the river would whisper to him as the distant stars and the ancient willow did.

Min watched the silent river. A great many men made their fortunes on the river. Min should give the idea some thought. That is what the village elders said, his neighbor Zixin first amongst them.

It had surprised Min when Zixin had offered advice. The older man had not exchanged two words with Min's father even though their houses stood side by side.

Min wondered what his father would say to that advice. Min would ask a priest to view his father's shrine and instruct him. It had been nearly a year since the funeral, and not once had Min's ancestor spoken. Min was surely doing something wrong. He could no longer feel his ancestors' presence in his home, nor sense the gentle wisdom of their guidance.

Once the rain passed, Min returned to his work. It was summer and the light yet good for hours.

Min worked as he always did, with his mind on matters unrelated to the cultivation of rice. He was born a rice farmer, as his father had been, and his grandfather. Like his father, Min had learned the work at an early age. His hands knew their business so that his mind did not need to dwell upon earthly matters. There existed a world of thoughts to chase, and no better opportunity to do so. Min did not feel the passage of time until the fading light slowed his hands and pinioned his coursing mind to the present.

His work done for the day, Min rested in the shadow of the ancient willow and watched the sun set in the west. The waning light painted the river red, the sun's arc retreating behind the distant shoreline with a speed that never failed to surprise him. Min watched a while longer, until the first fireflies began to spark.

He would tell Zixin that he did not want to abandon the land and make his fortune on the river. There was fortune enough for him here.

Min placed his palm against the willow's trunk and stood

silent for some time, listening to the nighttime world awaken. It had been a long day and he had worked hard. The evening remained warm. He might walk home in minutes, yet there existed nothing for him there. No glowing hearth. No dinner waiting. No smile in greeting. Without his father to look after, there was less than nothing. A hollow in which to lie.

Min stretched out beneath the willow and within minutes fell asleep.

And minutes later was awaked by the sound of rustling cloth.

A fine lady sat with her back to the willow trunk, her knees drawn up, her crossed arms wrapped about her legs.

Min leapt to his feet. "I beg your pardon. I didn't see—"

"Why do the birds flee?" He could tell from her voice she was born of quality and raised amongst her own kind.

"Which birds, great lady?"

"All of them," she said. "When the ice coats the river."

Min laughed. He'd been thinking about that very topic earlier in the day when he'd spied a duck out of season. "You mean why do they migrate?"

"Yes. I must so mean."

I have a theory," Min said. "But I should—"

She patted the earth beside her. "Sit. Tell me."

Min did sit, and he did tell her, and she asked him more questions. *Why are some days longer than others? How does one count grains of rice? What lies on the farther shore? Are there gods, and do they love us?*

He knew how one counted grains of rice, but as for the rest, her guess was as good as his. They talked the night through and at some time he must have dozed, for when he awoke she was gone.

He thought of her all the next day, and waited by the willow for her that evening, but she did not appear. For six nights he slept beneath the willow, dreaming of her. She did not appear.

After the seventh night he declared himself a fool and his vigil done.

He returned home to a cold hearth and an empty bed. Around midnight he took his bedclothes outside and lay beneath the stars. It seemed strange and terrifying to him that he had not known discontent until he had met her. His life had not changed. This night was no different than any other night since his father had died. He had not suffered a loss. Quite the opposite. He was richer from having met her, if only briefly. It was in his mind, in his *imagination*, that he had constructed something more for them. A hope. A wish.

There was no *them*.

In the morning Zixin stopped him and asked Min about his thoughts.

Min's brow wrinkled. "Regarding?"

"The river, and the vast opportunity it presents for a man of action."

"I'm yet considering the possibilities," Min said.

In truth he had very nearly made up his mind. If she would not come to him, he would go to her. He did not know where to seek her, either upstream or down, but seek her he would. He had been happy and now he was not.

In the end he did nothing. He went to work. He ate his lunch beneath the willow. When it rained, he took his ease beneath the willow. He passed the willow on his way home and placed his palm against its trunk, listening to the world. Life carried on around him. The river rolled past. The sun set and rose. The stars remained constant, but for one.

He did not forget her. If anything, she seemed more firmly fixed in his thoughts. He did not need to imagine a life without her. There could be none, so entwined were his own thoughts of his true life here, alone, and of *their* imagined life, here, together.

He rested his forehead against the ancient tree's trunk. "We will stay, you and I."

He arrived home later than usual that night, surprised to find a light in his home, and then angry when he imagined Zixin had not waited for Min to leave on the river before installing his surplus relatives in Min Sheng's house.

Min flung the door open, his accusing finger raised before him.

She bowed to him and welcomed him with a smile. "Dinner is waiting, husband."

Min did not question providence. He took his seat and gazed at her over his rice bowl, and resumed their discussion, beginning precisely where they had left off so many dark and empty nights before. "I am, upon reflection, swayed by your argument." *There were indeed gods, and they do love us.*

Min Sheng and Liu Xing Chen had many children and lived a joyous life together. The village prospered. There was great happiness. Their boys grew up straight and tall, their daughters beautiful and graceful. Their house grew crowded. The lane outside rang with laughter and the sounds of children at play.

Min Sheng's life changed little. He went to work. He ate his lunch beneath the willow. When it rained he took his ease beneath the willow. He passed the willow on his way home and placed his palm against its trunk, listening to the world. Life carried on around him. The river rolled past. The sun set and rose. The stars remained constant, but for one, which now glowered in the sky above.

Min Sheng did not notice the stars in the heavens. His gaze was all for Liu Xing Chen and the bright constellation that danced about her, tugging on her apron strings and begging for both their attention.

One day Min heard that the village elders had decided to build a quay so that ships of the river might dock and trade.

They had no wood some argued, but Zixin pointed out that the village did have a tree. Trees were made of wood.

It was decided to cut down the ancient willow in three days' time.

Min argued strongly against this, but Zixin's family had swelled in the village, and yet continued to arrive from upriver, their feet muddied from splashing through the shallows, their clothing soiled and sodden from clambering up the slippery riverbank to the road. These were city people, used to comfort, and they argued against Min, many voices against one.

Zixin took no part in the argument, except to say that the people had spoken. There would be a quay.

Min knew, everyone with sense knew, that though the ancient willow was tall and mighty, there was not enough clear wood in it to build a quay. The village would not have a quay, but the *start* of a quay, one of wood, wood that would rot away without the life force of the ancient willow's deep-sunk roots to nourish and sustain it. Min kicked a stone from the roadway and trudged home unsatisfied. There was no reasoning with Zixin. Min's neighbor had taken a disliking to Min Sheng since Liu Xing Chen's love had altered Min's fortune.

Min could not sleep. He tossed and turned in bed. He wondered why ships and quays were made of wood and roadways were not. The answer seemed obvious. *Because ships must float, and wood floats.*

Quays did not float.

Min leapt swiftly and silently from bed, and woke his children, one by one, careful not to wake Liu Xing Chen, who was with child and needed her sleep. He hushed them, and told them to dress. He led them out into the night and along the road until it branched toward the distant mountains. He told them what they must do in darkness, even the babes who had only recently begun to walk, and like dutiful soldiers, they nodded as one and marched off into the darkness.

Three nights they did thus.

When the village elders arrived, and while Zixin's clan, armed with axes and saws, were yet marching toward the ancient willow. Min approached and asked, respectfully, why one would wish for a quay of wood that might last a lifetime when one could have a quay of stone that would stand for a thousand years.

One said because they had no stone. Min pointed at the mountain in the distance. "We live in the shadow of stone."

Another said because the stone is distant, and heavy, and would take time to gather. Min pointed at the ancient willow. "Cutting down such a tree is hard work, and wet wood is heavy. It will be two seasons before it is dry enough to work."

Zixin had arrived by then and said, "This village does not own the mountain. The stone is not ours to do with as we please."

"But—"

"The people have spoken," Zixin said.

Min nodded, and bowed his head, and walked a dozen paces away. He clambered like a ram to the top of a heaping mound of stones, one that had not been there the night before. "One cannot argue with the people," Min said.

From his high vantage point Min could see the long line of carts, each loaded with stones, coursing along the road from the mountain. Min Sheng's children had raced the roadways by night, offering a cup of rice at each farmyard for every cart of stone between the river and the mountain. Farmers hated stone like Zixin hated another man's happiness. There was no end to the energy they would invest in seeing it gone from their lives.

Zixin picked up a stone. "Some of these are but pebbles."

"They are children of the mountain," one of Zixin's uncles, a stonemason from the city, said. "They are needed for a strong foundation." He ran his gaze over Min, his gaze narrowing. "How does a rice farmer know this?"

"He doesn't need to," Min said. "He has wise neighbors."

The uncle laughed, and said, "I will get my tools."

Zixin glared at Min before storming away.

The quay was built. People came and went. Not just those fleeing the cities, but boatmen, children of the river, who, like Min Sheng's family, had plied their trade for generations.

Unlike Ming Sheng's family, these poor souls had suffered misfortune. A tempest, a tidal wave, a drought, a flood, various tales of woe and loss, each distinct in detail but dreadfully similar in nature.

One day Min heard that the village elders had decided to build a boat. They had no wood for a boat, some argued, but Zixin pointed out that the village did have a tree. Trees were made of wood.

It was decided to cut down the ancient willow in three days' time.

Min argued strongly against this, but Zixin's family had overflowed the village, and yet continued to arrive from upriver, their houses crowded, their children restless and idle. There was no work that a boatman would not do for less.

The boatmen lived in squalor, ten families to a house, perhaps more. They could afford to slave beneath the sun for ten grains of rice a day, perhaps less. They were not respectable, settled people with standards to uphold and appearances to maintain.

"We know nothing of boatbuilding," Min said. "If we saved and pooled our excess, we could buy a boat. But if we do as you propose we will not have a boat, and we will not have a tree." His neighbors argued against Min, many voices against one. *We will have jobs. Good pay. Work for idle hands.*

"The people have spoken," Zixin said. There would be a boat.

"One big enough to carry all the boatmen away," the stone-mason said. He patted Min on the back as they both trudged home from the meeting. The stonemason had done well since the building of the quay. There were now stone buildings in the village, with more planned. "I can see it in your eyes," he said. "You are not defeated."

"Willow is not a proper wood for a boat," Min Sheng said. "Ironwood. Teak. These are what is needed."

"And how does a rice farmer know this?"

"His children know the children of boatmen."

"Do they also know the children of shipwrights?"

"Sadly, no," Min said. "We are laborers. The children of laborers do not mix with the children of craftsmen."

The stonemason grunted and walked beside Min in silence.

"It's a pity one can't build a ship of stone," he said.

"Indeed," Min Sheng said. "One might soon need a ship-yard, with so much traffic on the river, and so many desperate and idle hands about."

The stonemason laughed. "Ironwood and teak, you say?"

"So I have heard. Though I would ask a shipwright to be certain."

Min Sheng's life changed little. He passed the willow on his way home and placed his palm against its trunk, listening to the world. Life carried on around him. The river rolled past. The sun set and rose. The stars remained constant, but for one, which now stared down upon him night and day.

The sounds of the shipyard were distant from his door, yet he could faintly hear them working. There were many ships on the river now, and many boatmen, many hungry mouths to feed and bellies to fill.

Min had never worked harder in his life.

The village had grown.

His children had grown.

Liu Xing Chen had grown as well, more beautiful than when they had first met, and more deeply seated in his heart.

Min Sheng had what all men dream of, and few achieve. A

home. A family. Work that fulfilled him. Time to ponder the world around him. He could imagine no greater joy. No greater peace.

One day Min heard that the village elders had decided to build a temple, to please the gods and ward away the evil eye that hung overhead at all times. The star was brighter than the moon now, turning night into day and giving man or beast no rest.

In every village and in every city across the land a temple was to be built. Together the prayers of the people might prove sufficient. No small number of monks and priests had tried and failed.

There was strength in numbers.

In unity.

For once Min Sheng agreed. The village had gained many skilled craftsmen. He imagined a temple rising near the ship-yard, strong walls of stone, broad rafters of teak, tiled in red clay and cool in its shadow.

Min Sheng did not know the names of all the gods. He only knew that they loved him. They had sent him Liu Xing Chen. They had given him fine children. They had never asked more of him than he was able to give. A temple in their honor seemed little to ask.

Zixin was district magistrate now. He glanced from face to face before settling his gaze on Min Sheng. "The temple will be made of willow."

Min Sheng laughed. "One cannot build a temple of willow."

"One has. And anything *one* can do," Zixin said, "*Many* can do better. The work will take many hands. Many axes."

Min Sheng swallowed. "In three days—"

Zixin nodded and stifled a smile. "Today, Min Sheng."

"Just and merciful gods would not—"

Zixin shouted him down. "There are no such gods!" He

pointed toward the sky, where a second sun seemed to blaze beside the first. "Are you blind, fool?"

"But—"

"It is decided." Zixin crossed his arms and gazed from face to face. "The Emperor has spoken."

Min Sheng raced for his home, he pushed his way through the crowd of idlers and malcontents gathered to gape, past the boatmen with their axes and their apologies, past even the ancient willow without slowing, his fingers reaching for his doorway, the distant thud of axes striking his heart like blows, a stifled sob from within, "*Husband—*"

Liu Xing Chen was gone.

Min Sheng would never see her again.

Would never see the ancient willow again.

There would be no temple to any god.

Min Sheng gathered his children and took the first boat downstream.

He did not look back.

And he did not stop at the shoreline.

Min Sheng no longer dreams of the night sky, or of the stars.

His children, and Liu Xing Chen's, dance amongst the heavens.

Like raindrops on the river,

We, and they...

Are united.

35

Ciarán sat in silence for a long while before speaking. "That isn't the story those pictures tell."

"Of course it isn't," Wing said. "This book is not about Min Sheng and Liu Xing Chen."

"Then why did you—"

"This book is about their children." She flipped from page to page. "How they spread amongst the stars. How they build a new and better society. How they conquer their baser nature and thrive." She glanced at Ciarán. "But most of all? It is about how they honor their ancestors, not with words or prayers but with deeds. Have you not read it?"

"I've read it twice."

"Then you know."

"Know what?"

"Only a child of Liu Xing Chen could have written this story. Only a son or daughter of the willow wife."

"The *Willow Bride*."

"Being a daughter of Zixin, I do not know the difference between such words."

"You're a daughter of Zixin, the villain in the story?"

She laughed. "Zixin the villain? I think not."

"He is Min Cheng's enemy."

"He is Min Cheng's *rival*. Zixin is the captain, who, in the face of a typhoon, severs the ship's anchor chain to save the lives of all aboard. Without Zixin's goading Min Sheng would never have left the harbor."

Ciarán considered the idea. "Do you know the danger of being thought clever?"

"Do I?" Wing snorted. "It is this. One does not expect to meet another more clever."

"Cleverer," Ciarán said. That hadn't been what he'd been thinking, but, rather, sometimes a story was just a story and the simplest explanation the best.

"We agree," Wing said. "That is why this story, of Zixin and Min Sheng, has ended lives. When Zixin claims the emperor has spoken, is it true? Did the emperor command that the old ways be destroyed and thus untether the people from their ancient gods? Or did Zixin lie and claim the emperor's mandate as his own, betraying the duties of his station?"

"What do you think?" Ciarán said.

"I think it does not matter. In the judgement of such gods, both can be true. Zixin lied, and thus he and his descendants deserve death.

"Or, Zixin acted as the true voice of empire, and thus the emperor and his descendants deserve death. As do the emperor's servants, including Zixin and his descendants."

"In both cases the children of Zixin fare poorly," Ciarán said.

"We are empire," Wing said. "Even faring poorly, we do well."

"By 'we' you mean the Huangxu Eng."

"All Eng. Huangxu, Ojin, Alexandrian. This division is an artificial schema postdating the exodus from Earth. One's culture is difficult to separate from one's blood. There were disagreements, tribal in nature and entirely unscientific. We are genetically identical in all but the most superficial ways. Our practices differ. We appear to differ in material attributes. The shape of our eyes. The color of our skin.

"In spiritual terms we are all descendants of Zixin. We are all equally guilty. Zixin supplanted the last emperor, with or without the emperor's knowledge and approval."

"Do the not-Eng believe this?"

"No one *believes* this. Almost no one even considers it. We are superior to those beneath us and inferior to those above. That is what we *believe*. This distinction that there is more than one way to view the world is one only scholars of Zixin may consider. It is this renegade thought that marks us."

"Marks you for what?"

"Not *for* anything. *As* potential claimants."

"Claimants to the throne."

"Claimants to *supremacy*. The throne is nothing but an ornate chair."

"Why are you telling me this?"

"Because one cannot have *superiors*. *Rivals*, however, are very fashionable."

"Am I your rival?"

"The thought has occurred to me. But after viewing this book, I think you may be much more than that. Have you noticed the strangest aspect of the Zixin and Min Sheng myth?"

"Do I have to pick just one?"

Wing chuckled. "Liu Xing Chen's children—"

"They don't disappear or die like Liu Xing Chen does," Ciarán said. "When the willow is chopped down."

"Indeed. They are not demigods. But they are not entirely human, either. They are something new." She twisted in her seat to face him. "You are Liu Xing Chen's descendant. You are something new."

"It's a picture book," Ciarán said. "One with a story made up by—"

"Are you blind, fool?" She tapped her finger against a page. "What does this picture show?"

He glanced at the picture before quickly glancing away. "A wedding." Ciarán despised that illustration. He nearly tore it out of the book the first time he'd seen it. It did show a wedding, an old-style island wedding, one where the husband was Macer Gant and the bride Lorelei Ellis.

He had worked up the nerve to tell Laura how he felt about her when his mother's condition worsened. And then there wasn't time. And then the book. And that... He'd had the feeling that his mother had thought Laura and he would make a good match. The story in her death book seemed to say that. But the picture... Made the story a lie.

"You are the groom. I am the bride. Now we may get naked."

"That's not me in that picture. And that's not you."

"Then why does the man look like you, and why does the woman look like me? And wearing the shenyi of a scholar and the fengguan of a Zixin princess?"

"The man looks like Macer Gant," Ciarán said.

She tapped the page. "That is not you?"

"I wish it was."

"And the woman? Do you know another scholar-princess of Zixin?"

"It's a small island. There weren't that many..."

"What?"

"Girls," Ciarán said. "There weren't many people to use as models for pictures, boys or girls."

"Who is this Macer Gant?"

"Hang on." Ciarán flipped through the pages of the death book. There were only three models for all the action characters in the book. Macer, Lorelei, and him. It was clear the artist knew the difference between Macer and Ciarán. But every girl or woman in the pictures looked like Lorelei, except in the last picture, where the woman sinking beneath the waters of the Willow Bride looked like Ciarán's mom, before she'd grown ill.

Ciarán flipped back and forth from page to page. Out of the forty pictures ten had Lorelei in them. Of those ten only three had Macer in them, and in all three Lorelei was outfitted in traditional Huangxu Eng dress.

"The woman in these pictures isn't Lorelei Ellis."

"Clearly," Wing said. "She is a scholar-princess of Zixin. She is Wing."

"Possibly. Or someone like you. I can see that now."

"There is no one like Wing but Wing. Where can I find this Macer Gant?"

Ciarán reached into his pocket and removed a coin. It appeared to have the picture of an all-seeing eye on one side and the picture of a cat on the other. "Keep this with you at all times and he'll find you."

Wing studied the coin. "Do you think I am so easily tricked?"

"When you want to be," Ciarán said.

"Is Macer Gant also a descendant of Liu Xing Chen?"

"You know I've never really thought about it." Ciarán was descended from the *Willow Bride* crew on his father's side, and Macer on his mother's side. Of the three of them only Lorelei was a true child of the *Willow Bride*. It was easy to forget she'd been adopted by the Ellis, and wasn't his natural-born heir.

Of course, none of that mattered, unless he believed that the myth of Min Sheng and Zixin had some basis in literal truth, and that truth somehow related to the *Willow Bride*. That there was something... trans-human... about his family and their neighbors seemed far-fetched. He wouldn't discount the possibility that the myth had some basis in fact, though, just as he didn't discount stories of the Folk. He had no intention of using that speculation to inform his decisions, however.

Wing pocketed the coin. "I might have robbed you and taken that coin, unknowing."

"There are many things you might have done to me, and haven't."

"Dispose of you, for instance?"

"It happens with pirates and hijackers."

"You might prove useful in the future."

Ciarán nodded, and kissed the back of her hand. "Princess."

She tapped him on the forehead, and when he looked up, kissed him fully on the lips, stunning him for an instant, before biting his lip, and drawing blood.

"Do not pretend with me," Wing said. "You were not born to serve."

"Rivals then," Ciarán said.

"That." Wing ran her gaze over him. "If not something more. We will get naked, you and I. And when we do?" She grinned. "The heavens will tremble."

36

The cargo deck of the shuttle proved the only space large enough for the three to sit together and review notes. Maris Solon uncrated a portable holo tank on a tripod. Konstantine lashed it to the deck while Maris fiddled with her handheld.

A three-dimensional projection of a man appeared in the tank. He stood in League formal wear, his gaze narrowed, a thin smile on his lips. He had one hand hidden in his pocket. The other held a tall, narrow wine glass. He appeared to be about to say something cutting or witty, perhaps both. There was no hint of the wolf behind his eyes.

Konstantine settled into her seat. "He appears older now. When was this taken?"

Maris Solon perched on the edge of a jump seat. "At our wedding."

Konstantine snorted. "Come again?"

"Hector Poole and I were married shortly after the evacuation of Mera."

"This man is your husband?" Ciarán said.

"He was. For a short time," Maris said.

"Let me get this straight," Konstantine said. "You *married* the Dapper LT?"

"It seemed a good idea at the time. But that is beside the point. I want to make certain that we are all discussing the same man." She aimed her attention his way. "Ciarán?"

"It's him. That or a hound made from his pattern."

She raised a single eyebrow. "You do get around."

"Unfortunately."

"Helen?"

"Did he blackmail you?"

"He's amusing from a distance. Entertaining. But up close?"

"Not so much," Konstantine said.

Maris Solon smiled. "Quite the opposite, particularly... in private. But Hector is a complex man, and one is constantly aware that, even when alone with another, he is..."

"Performing for an audience," Ciarán said.

"You *have* met him," Maris said.

"I believe I must have."

"Then you know not to accept anything he says or does at face value."

"At two-faced value," Konstantine said.

"No," Maris said. "He's consistently opaque. But if you think you've caught him in a lie you are mistaken."

Ciarán cleared his throat. "These documents—"

"All genuine, I believe. They merely appear contrived because they're so complete and focused and tell their story so expertly. I believe it could be Hector that found the tag-end of this thread, but this doesn't look like his work. It's too..."

"Professional," Konstantine said.

"Too bloodless, on the one hand, and not bloody enough on the other. There is too much information and not enough bodies. I trust that Hector passed this information along, but he couldn't have compiled it. He is working with someone."

"Lord Aster," Konstantine said.

"Unlikely. This is the sort of information best held close and used. It isn't handed away to an agent of a foreign power."

"Aoife nic Cartaí isn't an agent of any power," Ciarán said.

Maris Solon leaned forward in her seat. "It wasn't handed off to her, now, was it?"

"He couldn't have known I'd—"

"Stop right there," Maris Solon said. "You must purge that idea from your mind." She leaned back in her seat. "Best you assume he does know and hasn't told you."

"On that first drop. The Dapper LT didn't know we'd be massacred."

"Did you check the ship's manifest, Pilot?"

"Why would I?"

"To count the body bags in ship's stores."

"There were eight dead. Eight bags."

"We had six bags on board, Pilot."

"Not on a vessel with a crew of eight, you didn't."

"We had two casualties the previous cruise. I'd requisitioned replacement body bags, but they hadn't arrived."

Konstantine's brow wrinkled. "I don't understand."

"Hector Poole brought spares," Ciarán said. "Expecting they might be used."

"He brought precisely two spares. Knowing they would be needed," Maris Solon said. "That is Hector Poole." She turned to Ciarán. "You didn't deny it."

"Being an agent of a foreign power?" He shrugged. "If all that documentation is true, I guess I am."

Konstantine's face paled. "Are you saying Karen is a spy? And I handed League intel to him?"

"I'm not a spy," Ciarán said. "But I appear to be an agent of a foreign power."

"*Quite Possibly Alien*," Maris Solon said.

"It thinks it's defending the League. When it learns that the League—"

"*When* it learns?" Maris Solon said. "Not if?"

"There are no secrets between us."

"Then it should know that this monstrous scheme... This is the work of a *cabal*. This isn't the League."

"Prove it," Ciarán said.

"I can't," Maris Solon said. "Not without telling you things I shouldn't. Things you won't believe."

"Try me."

"Do you believe that alien life exists?"

"I don't," Ciarán said.

"Then—"

"I know it does." He looked her in the eye. "And I have the scars to prove it."

She stared at him for the longest time before she spoke.

"Pilot, please leave us."

Helen Konstantine chuckled. "Like hell I will."

37

Ciarán opened the hanging locker and glanced inside, vacuum nozzle in his hand. "Huh." He switched off the vacuum cleaner, reached for his handheld, and rang Maris Solon.

"Kind of busy," Maris said.

"Did you unpack your luggage?"

"No. Can this wait?"

"It can." He reached into the locker and pulled out the pair of garments hanging there, dark blue utilities. What he imagined had once been called navy blues. They were devoid of ornamentation. One set seemed sized for Maris Solon. The other set seemed sized for him. They seemed a strange thing to find, but after everything he'd experienced, and everything Maris Solon had told him, somewhat anti-climactic. If Lord Aster and Hector Poole were the all-knowing masterminds Maris Solon claimed they were, they might have provided him a change of drawers and socks. Of course, you wouldn't keep those in the hanging locker, but in a spacer's locker under the bunk.

He'd needed to think about all he'd heard, and the cleaning, first pass anyway, was nearly done. Maris Solon's story filled in details of his own, and his of hers. He was still digesting it all, trying to puzzle out all the implications. Thinking while he worked was the best sort of thinking for that.

He dropped to his knees and glanced beneath the bottom portside bunk. Two spacer's chests, one filled with smalls and a new pair of hullwalkers for him, the other with the same for her.

He checked beneath the other bunk and found a matching set of storage trunks. The first seemed packed to overflowing with weapons and personal items, all in good condition. Modern, but not recent, the sort of kit a military officer might accumulate, along with the ribbons and medals beside them. The nerve disrupter atop it all seemed freshly minted and utterly unused. Why the ugly weapon lay dressed in a red ribbon and bow eluded him.

The second trunk was nearly empty. An overseer's rod. A pendant spire. A ball of augustinite.

And a merchant's license.

Ciarán blinked. He reached out and reverently lifted the card, flipped it over, and laughed.

If he'd never felt a real merchant's license, he might have been fooled. And it would likely pass inspection anywhere outside of the Federation. The merchant ring beside it, however, was the real deal. He slipped it on to see how it felt. Heavier than he'd expected. He took the ring off, and stowed all the personal gear, and finished his cleaning.

The hull remained a mess. It would take a work crew a week to do a proper job, but at least he wouldn't get filthy just walking about anymore. He dumped his utilities in the refresher, collected the new kit, and bare-footed it to the shuttle, whose cargo deck was large enough to stand upright in, and whose freshwater tanks were topped up. He showered under the hose-out reel, the wastewater gathering in the blood troughs and piped to the shipboard black tank. He'd begun to think he'd never feel clean again.

The five-minute claxon sounded as he was squeezing his way past the Templeman drive sphere. There was nowhere to belt down in the berthing compartment but in the bunk. He glanced toward the bridge, which only had seating for two.

The ladders.

He'd forgotten about them. They led to gun turrets according to Maris Solon. He hadn't cleaned them, hadn't even inspected them, because he wasn't going to be shooting any guns at anyone. Certainly not fifty- or sixty-year-old guns that hadn't seen a swab or a firing in all that time. And underwater for at least some of that time. He hadn't cleaned up there, or down there, and he had on his new fine clothes, but they did have seats, had to, and if he was going to pop from one universe to another, he'd like to do it slouching like a barbarian on a stolen throne, and not as cargo supine and lashed down like a corpse.

Up or down?

Ciarán chuckled.

Like there was ever any question.

He began to climb.

38

T he two-minute warning sounded. He hadn't cleaned the gun turrets, but someone surely had. Probably when they had replaced the guns. He recognized the manufacturer, Sturmvessen, but not the model. He had glanced through the manufacturer's catalog while shopping for kit for the Legion, but he clicked away when he made it to the price list. He could buy a longboat for less than the lowliest model in the line.

He belted in, careful to keep his hands and feet clear of anything that might accidentally wake the gleaming weapons.

The one-minute warning sounded, and he looked around for a get-sick bag.

There wasn't one.

Brilliant. And me in my shiny new clothes.

His guts roiled, his vision blurred, for ten, twenty, thirty seconds, and then it was over.

His belts were off, his feet on the ladder rungs, his hands on the rails, a short slide down spacer style. His hullwalkers slapped the deck and moved on in one fluid motion, impossibly right, and something Plowboy Ciarán couldn't have done. Not a year ago, nor six months ago. Not without falling on his face or breaking something expensive. He shoved through the flight deck curtain and peered out the forward viewports.

Hello, Persephone.

Konstantine twisted in her seat. "Who are you supposed to be?"

He handed her the merchant license.

She read it out loud. "Merchant Dermot Leprous, Leprous and Sons, *Impossible Bargains*, Contract Station."

"That's a typo," Ciarán said. "It should say Freeport Station." That it didn't meant Hector Poole was good, but he wasn't a mind reader.

Maris Solon swiveled in her seat. Her gaze seemed to focus on the pendant spire. "Does that hurt?"

"You get used to it." He glanced at the system scan. "Light traffic."

"No traffic," Konstantine said. "My vessel is parked on the ring. There's an in-system freighter three berths down and a third vessel hiding behind the planet."

"Hiding?"

"We're trying to get a drive signature off it."

"Can I use the comm while you do?"

Konstantine glanced at Maris Solon. "Captain?"

"So I'm back under orders now, am I?"

"I'm—"

"Belay that, whatever you meant to say. Take my seat, Merchant Leprous. It's a job for the expert systems now."

"I've laid out your kit," Ciarán said.

"My kit?"

"Shower's in the shuttle, the water's cold but wet."

"What precisely is wrong with my present appearance?"

"It's not the way you look, Your Grace." Ciarán winked. "They say even the queen sweats."

"She perspires," Konstantine said.

"She also bathes," Ciarán said. "Dump my kit out of the refresher if you prefer civilian garb. I have an identification card for you either way."

"Courtesy of Hector Poole, I presume."

"I think so."

"Who am I to be?"

"As a civilian, Penelope Leprous, Merchant Leprous's dowager mother. Traveling on a League transit-only card."

"Do I look like a Penny to you?"

"Like a bad one," Konstantine said.

"And the other?"

"Admiral Maris Solon. Technical Advisor and Superintendent of the Academy."

"For?"

"The Legion of Heroes, an independent mercenary company operating out of the Contract System, Huangxu Contested Space."

"Under what flag?"

"It is a mercenary company," Ciarán said. "The flag doesn't matter."

"Under what flag is the company chartered?"

"The Eight Banners Empire."

"What the hell, Ciarán?"

"They waived all registration fees."

"I'll look like a traitor."

Ciarán said nothing.

"My credentials?"

"Transit only—"

"Lovely."

"Transit only, restricted."

"That's absurd. Restricted to what?"

"From what. No travel to or from the Home Worlds."

Maris Solon's jaw worked. She stared into the distance.

"Very well."
She elbowed him out of the way.

39

Maris Solon stormed onto the bridge in her Legion of Heroes utilities, her hair yet wet. When she spoke, her voice was like a flail, one she tapped against her wrist while she decided which idiot deserved the flogging. "Why are we ballistic?"

"Two reasons." Ciarán pointed at the command display. He handed her his handheld.

"Did you use the comm?"

"Nearly. But the drive signature solution popped up before I keyed the system active."

"That mistake is on me," Maris said. "There is an annunciator for shipboard maneuvering, Pilot."

"It's not tied into the shuttle, Captain."

"Then you open the hatch and shout."

"That's what I told him," Konstantine said. "And he said, and I quote, 'She might yet be in a state of undress.'"

"I was soaped up and naked as the day I was born. I nearly broke my neck when the drive cut off." She aimed her finger at Ciarán. "Grow up. I'd rather you ogle me bare-assed than the undertaker. What is this? Some sort of joke?"

"I thought the inertial dampers—"

"This is a warship, not some breakbulk rubbish hauler. Now answer me."

"The drive signature matches the League vessel *Ibex*. The vessel's transponder is presently inactive, however *Radiance*, an undocumented vessel, has been logged as entering the system."

"No record of it leaving," Konstantine said. "And it's not showing up on the status board."

"I can see that. That vessel can't be *Ibex*. She was scuttled in the Alexandrine a half century ago."

"Maybe someone lied," Ciarán said. "And—"

"I was there when it happened."

"Did you see the flash?" Ciarán said.

"Of course not. I was in an escape pod. I'd lost my arm and a great deal of blood. But I was lucid through the entire affair."

"Then the expert system is wrong," Ciarán said. "I'm not sure it matters. Look." He pointed at his handheld.

"What am I looking at? A treatise on sensors?"

"It's a personnel tracker," Ciarán said. "Built to look like a library book on sensors. We use it aboard *Quite Possibly Alien*."

There were two dots on the display. There should have been only one.

"The designations?"

"One of them is mine." He tapped the display. "This one."

"Then your tracker is broken. It shows you as being on the station."

"That's Wing. I gave her my coin as a... token of esteem."

"And the other?"

"Maura Kavanagh. Her coin is on that unidentified hull."

40

Maris Solon looked up from the display. "That is *Ibex*. Though I don't see how it can be." She tapped her finger against the console. "Pilot, when is the last time you fired a weapon in anger?"

"I've never done that," Konstantine said. "I've been a transport pilot my entire career."

"Ciarán?"

"I'm not sure. How long's it been since I put out Admiral Shi's eye?"

"I mean a real weapon."

"I think the Admiral would back me up when I tell you. A blowgun dart is a real weapon."

"Shipboard weapons."

"We don't have those in the Federation."

She glared at him. "I've heard that lie before. On *Quite Possibly Alien*, then."

"It's bristling with shipboard weapons, except the crew doesn't get involved in their operation. The spiders do all of that."

"Spiders."

"The luminaires. Independently operating fragments of the ship's consciousness, or of the ship minder's consciousness, depending upon the task. The ship's minder works the weapons. Using the spiders as vectors of control."

She stared at him.

"They're also weapons themselves." Ciarán swallowed. "The spiders, I mean."

"It's a disturbing ship," Konstantine said.

Ciarán peered at the in-system plot. "Is it a dangerous ship, the *Ibex*?"

"A fast courier; all engine, no armor, no weapons, a crew of six plus."

"Plus what?"

"A diplomat."

"Maybe we should just talk to them then."

Maris Solon nodded. "We will. But first we're going to break their legs."

The comms console barked. Konstantine kicked it silent. "Automated distress call."

"Brilliant," Maris Solon said. "From?"

Konstantine chuckled. "*Ibex.*"

"Notify the locals, Pilot. We will handle this. Skip jump us to within one hundred meters of the hull."

"It could be a trap."

"Then we'll slag them," Solon said. "Slave the ship's guns to my exo and hold us stationary once in position."

"Roger that, Cap."

"Let's roll, *Knight Commander.*"

Ciarán raced along behind her as she headed aft. Maris Solon was much smaller than him, and it was hard to keep up with her in the skinny parts. "It's not like I chose that moniker," Ciarán said, as the shuttle's cargo hatch opened.

41

They hand-lined over. Maris Solon aimed her exo's weapon at the hatch controls.

"Wait," Ciarán said. "Did you really serve on this vessel?"

"I did. Very early in my career."

"Try your credentials."

The hatch cycled.

"That's why Federation vessels don't have guns," Ciarán muttered. *We'd come to rely upon them.*

"I didn't hear that."

"Stay behind you," Ciarán said. "If it's in front of you ignore it. If it's behind you, kill it."

"Got it in one, son."

"If Maura Kavanagh is in front of you? Don't kill her."

"How will I know her?"

"She'll let you know."

42

"That's distressing," Maris Solon said. "It looks like a shrapnel grenade went off in here."

It didn't. It looked worse. Like someone, or something, had gone through the crew like a typhoon of razor-sharp rage. "Power down your weapon, Maris," Ciarán said. "Do so now."

"I'm not powering down anything until I clear this hull. I've got enough limbs and torsos for four over here. What's your count?"

Ciarán tossed his own weapon down and wrenched his helmet off. He shouted. "Do it! Power down! That is an order!"

"Good lord." Maris Solon's armored exoskeleton turned toward him. "It looks like something's been *eating* them."

The briefest flicker of movement danced behind Maris Solon. The most perfect weapon ever devised stepped from the shadows.

Ciarán knew that was what she was. She had told him herself.

"Maura."

She wet her lips. "Plowboy. What brings you here?"

"Just passing."

Maura Kavanagh's torn utilities were caked with blood. There was blood on her face. On her hands. In her hair. She held her left hand on her right shoulder to keep the fabric of her utilities from falling away.

Something brushed against Ciarán's thigh.

Brushed against his thigh and purred.

"You'll need to make your mind up now, Maris Solon." Ciarán stared at the featureless surface of the exo's helmet. "You'll either take a lawful order from the Knight Commander of the Legion of Heroes or not. I don't blame you if you choose not to."

The suit's enunciator spoke. "What was that? Something *bumped* me."

"Ship's cat," Maura said. "When they... took me. Wisp followed me aboard."

"And then?" Ciarán said.

"They stuffed me in cryo. They thawed me out less than an hour ago, when they grew bored from waiting. I didn't know they were waiting for you until... Until... These aren't good people."

"Understood." Ciarán glanced about. "Is that all of them?"

"The captain," Maura said. "He's in... his cabin."

"Is he dead?"

"Not quite. But he's like his ship," Maura said. "Unmanned."

"Admiral Solon," Ciarán said. "See to the prisoner."

Maris Solon took two steps sternward and glanced into the single cabin. She raised her weapon and fired.

"I meant secure him," Ciarán said.

"I know you did," Maris said.

Ciarán glanced about. "Is there an autodoc on board?"

"Used to be," Maris said. "In case a diplomat got a hangnail."

"I don't need that," Maura said.

"Come here," Ciarán said.

Maura Kavanagh did as ordered for once.

Ciarán wrapped his arms around her. He brushed her hair back and kissed her forehead.

"No autodoc. And the cryo chamber is toast." Maris watched them, together. "Is she snoring?"

"Sobbing," Ciarán said. "It's Wisp that's snoring."

43

The Persephone system stationmaster seemed pleased to learn that she didn't need to dispatch a rescue vessel. *Ibex* had been running a false transponder, *Radiance*, out of Columbia Station, a rich son's private yacht, a toy. While under other circumstances the stationmaster might wish to investigate, given Merchant Leprous's obvious Freeman accent, the fact that a Freeman spacer needed autodoc hours, and Merchant Leprous was willing to ignore the embargo and pay cash for the hours, softened her heart and stayed her hand.

Persephone wasn't a frontier world, and it wasn't a home world but something in between: a close-in and marginally habitable system cursed by bad celestial mechanics. The planet had an eccentric orbit, one that caused it to have a pleasant spring, an idyllic autumn, a bitter winter, and a lethal summer.

No amount of terraforming could correct for bad geometry. They had tried for more than a century to solve the problem before giving up. One of the earliest worlds settled, six thousand years later Persephone was essentially an annual garden, one tended by those with deep family roots. The system was otherwise populated by timeshare developers, remittance men, and those who wished to disappear.

With enough stores laid in, Persephone's summer proved survivable in structures beneath the surface. The alternative for the bulk of those who remained in Persephone system was to spend the spring and autumn on the planet and summer on Persephone Station, an odd, T-shaped powered platform that followed an augmented orbit placing it nearer to the planet during the seasonal evacuations and further during the rest of the local year. There remained traffic up and down to the surface during the winter, which some hardy souls found tolerable on the surface.

It happened to be local spring, thus the station was nearly abandoned, but for those businesses and institutions seated on the station itself.

One of those institutions was the Diaspora Remembrance Society, a quasi-governmental organization that cataloged and collected source material related to the exodus from Earth over six thousand years earlier, and which claimed to "chronicle the subsequent diaspora of the people of Earth." While there could be found some material on the Eng role in the forced migration, the bulk of the collection remained focused on the League's role, and the production of reports and documents designed to keep the topic, and thus the Diaspora Remembrance Society, in the public eye.

The Remembrance Library Project housed the largest collection of "generation books," death books by another name, in the universe. That the Project housed the only such library seemed, at first to Ciarán, to overstate the collection's importance; however, the Society did claim to possess more than fifty million such books, which Ciarán decided had to be a typographical error—until he discovered that the trunk of the station's *T* was entirely dedicated to the collection and its caretakers. What had once been thousands of housing units for settlers were now dedicated entirely to a volunteer staff and the unread diaries of the dead.

Konstantine's stolen troop carrier lay moored at what passed for a ring on the station. A pair of docks sat empty between it and the only other vessel presently at the station, a well-worn in-system freighter from the looks of it.

Durable's airlocks weren't compatible with the station without an extended boarding tube. Maris Solon said that there was a tube on board, but it was likely unserviceable. They would need to shuttle over to the station.

Ciarán recognized the lie when he heard it. He asked her if, when he talked to the station, the lie should be heard or unheard.

She chewed her lip for a moment. "What would the Merchant Leprous do?"

"The Merchant Leprous does not have guns that could rake the station, or threaten the vessels docked nearby. The Merchant Leprous does, however, have a ship's cat on board, one that might choose to repel boarders or range about the station unseen."

"And who might delay us, if she were roaming, and we needed to depart."

Ciarán liked the easy way Maris Solon had shifted her thinking to align with his own, referring to Wisp not as *it* but as *her*, and the unstated rule that Wisp would not be left behind under any circumstances.

"Do we intend to rake the station?"

"I'd like to retain the option."

"Would you prefer the stationmaster perceive this?"

"They'd have to be pretty dense not to."

"Unless it seemed clear that our interest lay, not with the station, but with the vessel docked at it."

"If we told her that she'd never believe it."

"Then we will not tell her that. She will tell herself that."

"You can make her do that?"

Ciarán thought about it. After nearly three hundred years of discussion, this remained one of the central topics of disagreement at the Merchant Academy. Was what the Academy taught just force by another name?

A corollary of the Freeman Oath was a prohibition on the non-retaliatory use of force. Fraud by guile was considered force. Was persuasion taken to the level of art, and practiced on the unsuspecting, also force?

"I cannot bend her to my will," Ciarán said. "I can, however, make it difficult for her to do otherwise without conscious consideration." He glanced at Maris Solon. "So long as we are not interrupted."

"Why are you talking like that?"

"Like what?"

"Like a machine."

"He does that," Konstantine said. "When he's on the clock. They all do it somewhat, but Karen is the worst."

Maris Solon glanced at Konstantine. "Who are *they*?"

"Freeman Merchants. They talk all formal when they're working."

"Words are tools," Ciarán said. "They require care."

Maris Solon chuckled. "You people are weird. Tell the stationmaster we're going to slag that transport unless we get what we want."

"From?"

"From Wing. We'll leave the station out of it," Maris said. "All we want from the station is the autodoc hours. I'd prefer to shuttle over for those, with a full detail, but since I don't have a full detail, we'll bring the ship's cat, if she's amenable. Shirt-sleeves, like tourists, armed but no exos."

"There's an autodoc on the transport," Konstantine said.

"There isn't," Maris said. "I checked the ship's specifications."

"There's the one the Skinnies brought on board. They dumped Shi out of it before they stuffed him in the escape pod. I watched them."

"Ciarán?"

"I have negotiated with the station for autodoc hours. So long as we pay..."

"We'll pay. Work your magic, Merchant Leprous."

44

Maris Solon chuckled. "That was unbelievable."

Ciarán scrubbed his palm across his face. "It doesn't always go that well." He blinked and reached for the juice bulb he'd stashed beneath the comms console. "I think it's the utilities."

"They do fit well," Konstantine said.

"It's not that," Ciarán said.

"Isn't it?" Maris Solon said.

"In part, perhaps." But he doubted that very much.

"You look like a poster boy for the rugged individualist navy."

"Exactly," Ciarán said. "I look like I'm in the navy."

"That's your takeaway from that sentence?"

"It is. You could have said anything. I know what I look like. I've been called that before. But no one has ever mistaken me or any other Freeman for an *organization man.*

"The color. The cut. The lack of adornment. I don't know what it is. But she *was not* responding as she should have to Merchant Leprous. She was reacting to a powerful symbol. Something that has deep cultural meaning to her."

"Like Freemen and cat pictures," Konstantine said.

Ciarán laughed. "You're joking, but you nailed it. Precisely like that."

"Whatever it is, it worked," Maris said. "Now do Wing."

"I'll need to change first. What's cheese to a Leagueman will be chalk to her. And I'll need to shuttle over and talk to her in person. I'll take Maura with me."

"Don't you ever turn it off?" Maris Solon said.

Ciarán looked her in the eye. "You'll know it when I do."

"Did I miss something?" Konstantine said.

"Merchant Leprous wants to shuttle over. He's under the impression I'll think twice about slagging that hull with him on board."

"Is he right?"

Maris Solon locked gazes with him. "Go change."

Ciarán considered his options.

He turned toward the console and keyed the comms active.

"We will try it your way, Ship's Captain."

"Wing," Ciarán said.

The young woman smiled back at him from the display. "Ciarán. You look well."

"And yourself."

Ciarán leaned forward in his seat. "Did you miss me?"

"Not at all. I knew you would follow."

"My book."

"Sold, I'm afraid."

"I see. The gems?"

"Oh, I still have them. They are available."

"The autodoc?"

"Also available, for a price. I am open to offers."

"How are you finding the ship?"

"Spacious, though sluggish." She leaned toward the optics. "Confidentially?"

"Of course."

"I've stolen better."

Ciarán smiled. "So have I."

"I have not heard this."

"Do you recall the name of the buyer?"

"For your book? I may recall the name, address, and id addy."

"May?"

"I shall scour my memory, should we strike a bargain." She tapped her forehead. "It is here."

"Then we have a bargain, if you wish."

"I wish. Wing out."

The display went black.

Ciarán unbelted and stood. "I need to check on Maura."

Maris Solon blocked the corridor. "What just happened?"

"What did you think would happen? I've gotten you everything you asked for, Ship's Captain. Other than my retrieving my mother's death book, we are done here. Now please excuse me."

"How?"

"By making a poor bargain. I might have accomplished more in person but not over the comms. We would have ended up at the same place, but I believe I could have convinced her to exchange the book and autodoc hours for a speedy closing."

"She said she sold the book."

"In case you haven't noticed, Ship's Captain, people lie. And even when they don't, they tell half-truths. When someone like Wing says they sold the book it means they've sold the book. It does not mean they've delivered the book or received payment for the book."

"Noted," Maris Solon said. "But I'm still not clear on what we've offered them in return."

"*We* haven't done anything. *I've* traded her *Ibex* for the troop transport and those particulars mentioned."

"What? You can't do that."

"Don't I know it. Now if you'll excuse me, I need to go talk to Maura and see what she'll take for the vessel."

"It's a League vessel!"

"It' a Freeman prize vessel, taken during a war the League started."

"We answered the distress call," Konstantine said. "Doesn't that make it *our* prize?"

"It would," Ciarán said, "If Maura and Wisp hadn't taken control of the vessel before we arrived. Check the logs. She cleared the distress call before we touched the hatch."

"Do you have any idea what that vessel is worth?"

"I do now. By definition, it's worth exactly what I got for it."

"We're not doing this."

"We are exactly doing this. Word of a merchant." Ciarán looked Maris Solon in the eye. "Do I tell you how to drive the ship?"

"Not yet."

"Not ever."

"You're angry because—"

"I'm not angry," Ciarán said. "I'm explaining. Do not stand between me and mine. *Ever*. Now *faugh a ballagh*!"

Maris Solon stepped aside.

"Karen," Konstantine said.

"What?"

"She'll be okay. Maura's strong."

"I'll tell her you said so."

"You're strong too."

He turned at that, and their gazes met, and held. "I am informed, Pilot. Thank you."

Konstantine made a shooing motion. A tear traced its way along her cheek. "Go."

45

T he atmosphere of Persephone Station had a faint aroma of flowers. It might be that Aoife nic Cartaí could identify the scent, but it wasn't one Ciarán knew. The station was ancient, large, and empty, the architecture clearly League in nature but more ornate than was the current fashion—as if someone had languished time and love in every detail. It was no wonder the station hadn't been abandoned as a failure. There was too much hope and energy invested in it. One didn't discard art.

Ciarán wasn't entirely familiar with the layout of the station yet, but he had been on board several times since they'd arrived. The autodoc that they had agreed to pay for turned out to be the latest model, one far superior to the unit aboard the troop transport. And the facility was staffed—or, rather, over-staffed for the season, with highly qualified attendants. A physician had checked in on Maura twice, an unexpected luxury provided without charge by the stationmaster. Ciarán appeared to have made a more favorable impression that he had imagined.

Ciarán had followed Wing and her crew earlier in the day,

thinking to disrupt the delivery of his mother's death book to its buyer. The League was yet at war with the Huangxu Eng, though they'd ceased active hostilities at the request of the Eight Banners Empire. The trio of Mighty Eighty-Eights wore their harvest celebration costumes; a statuesque golden hind striding forward flanked by the towering silver antlers of the stags that paced her.

When he discovered who the buyer was Ciarán changed his mind. He lounged in the shadows until the exchange was complete, and then followed the buyer, first to an arcade beverage seller, and then to a block of apartments in the library section of the station. He noted the apartment number before returning to the ship for trade goods and backup.

The ship's captain was loath to leave the ship, and both Konstantine and Wisp were napping together. Out of all *Quite Possibly Alien*'s crew Konstantine had long been Wisp's favorite. The ship's pilot and the ship's cat could often be found in the same compartment either having a meal, playing catch, or simply hanging out together. If anything ever happened to Ciarán he knew where Wisp would end up, loved and cared for. It was great comfort to have such friends and allies. He hadn't realized how much he'd come to depend upon the crew until he'd been separated from their company.

It appeared Wisp felt the same way. She had missed Helen Konstantine as much as Konstantine had missed her.

When Ciarán left the ship Maura Kavanagh walked beside him. It wasn't a familiar feeling, having her near, but it felt right. It felt preordained, if one believed in such things.

Ciarán glanced at *Quite Possibly Alien*'s navigator. "Do you recall when we first met?"

"When you 'rescued' me, you mean?"

"I thought I was doing the right thing."

"You were," Maura said.

"You didn't need my help."

"You didn't do it for me. You did it for someone in need. Someone vulnerable. Someone alone. Someone without a crew, on a strange deck, under a strange sun."

"Later, I spit on your hullwalkers."

"I haven't forgotten."

"Do you recall what you said?"

"You'll polish those."

"Do you know what I did last night?"

"You polished my hullwalkers. The medical staff told me."

"They didn't."

"They did. Do know what I thought?"

"That you could do a better job?"

"Natch." She took his hand, stopped, and faced him "I thought, I'm glad I met you, Ciarán mac Diarmuid, on that deck, under that sun. I thought you were a fool playing at being a hero."

"You were right."

"I was. But I'd gotten you all backwards." She gazed along the block of apartments. "Now what are we doing here?"

"I'm going to meet a man. And you're going to keep me from killing him."

"Why would I do that?"

"As a favor to me."

"Like the favor you did me, trading away my new starship for some autodoc hours I didn't use?"

"Like that."

"Fine."

THE OLDER, slightly overweight man answered the door in course brown monk's robes. He ran his gaze over Maura and smiled. He glanced at Ciarán, and Ciarán broke his nose, shoving him into the apartment and forcing him to his knees. Maura entered and closed the door behind her.

Luther Gant spit out a mouthful of blood before mouthing the words Ciarán was thinking.

"Isn't this a coincidence."

"It is." There was no such thing as a *good* coincidence. "My book?"

"In the bedroom."

"I'll look," Maura said.

"Don't. He could see the book on a worktable beneath a viewscreen on the far wall. It wasn't a big apartment, two rooms, a galley, and a head. The bedroom door lay closed. Both it and the larger multi-purpose room beside it were sandwiched between the inner hull and a long featureless corridor. The fixtures and decorations were designed to mimic planetary standards. The bedroom door seemed just a door and not an airlock.

Ciarán pulled Luther Gant upright and marched him to the kitchen table. Made him sit. He pulled a necklace of pendant spires from his pocket and slapped it on the table. Ciarán knew instantly that Gant recognized them.

"What's in the bedroom?"

"Killers."

"Why aren't you dead?

"Why aren't you?"

"Why aren't you dead on Trinity Surface?"

"Because I know how to fake a death. You'd think that was obvious from the first time I faked a death."

"What are you doing here?"

"That Leagueman, pal of Olek's. Said if he ever had to hide out he was coming here. So I looked into it. He was right. It's a good bolt hole."

"Until now."

"Bad luck," Luther Gant said.

"And about to get worse. If I touch that book under the window?"

"If you or anybody touches it, they'll know."

"And come out of the bedroom."

"Or out of the wall next to the worktable. There's a hidden hatch."

"That leads to where?"

"The space between the inner and outer hulls."

"These friends of yours."

"They're no friends of mine. I'm the *bait*, lad. Have you not figured that out yet?"

A key scratched in the apartment door lock.

Maura and Ciarán stepped out of sight.

A small herd of deer entered, weapons drawn.

The golden hind spoke. "These bearer bonds you traded us are worthless."

"That's because the book you gave me is a fake."

The trio dropped their disguises. Fang closed the door and locked it. Zhao began to cross the compartment. Wing glanced around the compartment. Blinked.

"Ciarán."

"Wing."

"You know her?" Maura said.

All three aimed their weapons at Maura.

"You know her too. You sold her a starship."

"I practically gave it to her, you mean."

Wing grinned. "I prefer to think I stole it."

"Zhao," Ciarán said. "Don't touch the book."

Luther Gant had begun to rise.

"Sit," both Wing and Ciarán said as one.

"My book?"

"Aboard the transport," Wing said. "Consider it a kickback. Our new vessel is truly an impossible bargain."

"That's grand," Maura muttered.

Wing considered Luther Gant. "Is he a wanted man?"

"I can't think of a less wanted man."

"Then you can have him. Once he pays us."

Gant snorted. "Pay you? For a fake?"

"I prefer to think of it as an artist's tribute."

"I prefer to get back to our ship," Ciarán said. "We're done here."

"What about these killers?" Maura said.

"We can kill them later," Ciarán said. "Lets—"

"There are killers?" Wing said.

"In the bedroom," Maura said. "And in the walls."

"How many?"

"Ten or twelve."

"Which is it?"

"Twelve," Luther Gant said.

"In exos?"

"Hardsuits."

Wing grinned. "Excellent."

Fang and Zhao both sighed.

"Ciarán," Wing said. "Old man, and glittery woman. Clear the compartment."

"Suits," Luther Gant said, as he rose from his seat.

"Sit," Maura and Ciarán said as one.

"They're part of that crew from *Ibex*," Maura said. "You know it and I know it."

"They can't be. There's no room aboard that vessel."

"Then another vessel. Or local mercenaries."

"They're navy," Luther Gant said. "And not from around here."

Ciarán pulled his handheld free and hailed *Durable*. He asked Maris if there was a vessel docked nearby that could take a crew of twelve. She said there was. An in-system freighter.

"One big enough to ship a Templeman drive?"

"Oh, yeah," Maris said. "I can run an active scan. But when I do, they'll know."

"Don't do that. What is your expert assessment, based on the data you have?"

"My gut tells me it's a Q-ship. It shifted docks last night. Local freighters don't do that."

"We're engaging twelve hostiles in hardsuits," Ciarán said. "Where's Konstantine?"

"On the troop carrier."

"We'll try to herd them outside. I want at least one of them alive."

"That complicates things."

"Agreed," Ciarán said. "But I have a plan."

46

C iarán opened the bedroom door and stepped inside. They weren't trying to kill him, but to capture him, and they surely had tech that would recognize Maura and him on sight.

They turned out to be a single hard-suited spacer armed with a stunner. Their attention shifted to Maura when she stepped into the compartment holding a nerve disrupter and they wasted a second or two, holstering the stunner rather than dropping it, and another second bringing a plasma rifle to bear.

Long enough. More than long enough for the monomolecular whip of an overseer's rod to lick out and shear through the rifle's barrel just forward of the pre-heater reservoir. Ciarán didn't know what would happen after a trigger pull, and neither did the spacer, who hesitated long enough for Wing to reach forward, and press her bang stick stunner to the helmet's face shield and trigger it. The shield shattered as she rammed the rod forward and triggered it again, releasing her grip as the spacer slumped to the deck. The hidden hatch in the bedroom began to open and Zhao fired a pulse rifle through the crack. It sounded as if Fang had done the same in the adjacent room.

Wing rushed the bedroom hatch just as Ciarán kicked the hatch closed.

Station alarms began to sound, sensors tuned to detect weapons fire and alert the authorities. In moments League uniformed police would be racing toward the compartment.

Ciarán held up his finger for silence, and dropped to his knees beside the downed spacer and shook out a centimeter of the rod's whip. He plunged the whip into the hardsuit's breast-plate, severing the leads of the suit's health monitoring nexus. He twisted the spacer's neck so he could read the suit's vital signs display. He shoved his hand inside the helmet and toggled the suit's comms active.

"He's flatlined," Ciarán lied. "We need to capture another."

"We're going in," Wing said.

"Don't," Ciarán said. "I'll call the stationmaster and have her call a lock down. We don't want them getting away."

Ciarán gripped his handheld just as Maris Solon spoke.

"We've got squirters."

Ciarán sat down next to the unconscious spacer. He verified that the suit's vitals monitor remained offline and the comms open. "How many?"

"Ten," Maris said. "Make that eleven. They're heading for a freighter two berths down."

"Slag it," Ciarán said.

"Slag a freighter attached to a League station? Hang on. Now they're moving toward the troop transport."

"I said slag the freighter."

"I'm not firing on a freighter."

"That's a direct order."

Maris chuckled. "Now they're moving back toward the freighter."

"Ship's captain—"

"I do have a perfectly good pair of Sturmvessens I've never fired."

"Fire them," Wing said.

"I'd fire them," Maura said.

"Fine," Maris said. "I'll slag the freighter." She chuckled. "After they're all back on board."

"I need a survivor," Ciarán said.

"That might be a little tough," Maris said. "The freighter just tore free of the dock. It's backing off and firing on the squirters."

"Ping the freighter, Maris."

"Done. It has a Templeman drive. I can't fire on it this close to the station."

"Follow it out. Light it up, and finish this."

"Looks like six of the squirters might make it to the troop transport."

"On it. We're heading that way."

"Double time it, the drive is hot. If they have a pilot—"

"Understood. We're on it. I want that freighter, Ship's Captain."

"Roger that. Solon out."

Ciarán reached inside the spacer's helmet and keyed the transmitter off. He stood and lifted the prisoner by the accessory belt, slinging him over his shoulder.

He took the necklace of pendant spires from Luther Gant's fingers. "The Stationmaster's asked for these."

Luther Gant gazed up at Ciarán, and for the first time Ciarán realized Luther Gant was *old*. The man had remained forever frozen in a fifteen-year old's memory, a big man, powerful and overbearing.

"I need to tell the boy," Luther said.

"He's not a boy."

Their gazes met.

"Neither are you," Luther Gant said.

"I'm not."

"Will you tell Macer I'm not dead?"

"Do you want me to?"

"I guess not." He pulled his gaze away. "I never imagined you'd grow up to be the hard one."

"I never imagined I'd need to. Who told you to buy that book?"

"No one had to tell me. The Society pays top dollar, and they don't even read the blasted things. There's a raft of knowledge in these old books, the ones a man can decipher. And both the ones I can and can't read, I scan and sell on copies to people who can read them. It's entirely commercial, and highly profitable, so long as I can keep myself inserted between the seller and the Society. Buy low and sell high, and you wouldn't believe the margin."

"There is still the matter of the replica, and payment," Wing said.

"I don't have the money at the moment."

"I'll take it," Ciarán said. "Send me the bill."

"It is quite expensive."

"What isn't nowadays?"

"Friendship," Wing said. "The price is the same as it ever was."

Ciarán smiled. "Word of a Merchant." He hitched the prisoner higher onto his shoulder and told himself he wasn't born a fool. He was worse, the self-made kind. "Grab your kit, Mr. Gant. We'll give you a lift back to the land of the living."

47

C iarán leaned back in *Durable*'s first officer's seat and watched the recorded optical feed from the troop transport. He'd witnessed the aftermath, but he wanted to watch the play-by-play. Maris Solon said it was worth viewing. He could turn the sound off after the two-minute mark, if he liked.

They came in through the main hatch, six of them in hardsuits. They fanned out, three heading for the bridge, the rest searching the drop modules. Twenty seconds later two of them return dragging Helen Konstantine. She shrugged them off and stood her ground. One of them backhanded her, and she rocked on her feet but remained standing.

"The codes, granny," he said, and they all laughed.

Their hands were shaking though, hardsuits rattling as they considered what had just happened. Their own people hadn't simply abandoned them. They'd fired on them and taken out half their company. Not accidental friendly fire, but murderous fire, fire designed to silence them when it became clear they were to be left behind.

The third to go forward returned, excited. "The boards are live. She forgot to peg them."

"Senile *and* ugly," one said.

"Maybe she was napping," another said.

"I wasn't," Konstantine said. "I was on duty. Just... preoccupied."

She rubbed her fingers together, like she was trying to wipe something off them.

Something tarry and black.

"Preoccupied with what," one said. "Changing your runabout's oil?"

They all laughed.

"Show her the airlock," the leader said.

"I've seen it," Konstantine said. "It's on my ship. You've had your fun. Now put your weapons down."

"Put them down or what?"

"Or I'll send you to hell. When I was a girl they told stories about Karen, hell's boatman. All my life I'd thought Karen was a dog man. Turns out that was a lie."

The cabin went black.

"She's a cat fancier," Konstantine said. "Now put your weapons down and surrender."

A loud thump sounded.

A series of quiet clicks began in the distance.

The clicks grew nearer.

The night-vision optics powered up, the ship's cabin becoming a black and green netherworld.

A voice on the edge of panic spoke "Is that Karen?"

"Charon, you idiot," another said. "Now calm down. He's a myth."

"You'll wish she was. That's not Karen stalking you." Konstantine glanced up at the sensors and smiled. "It's her shadow. Now put your weapons down while you still can."

The optical feed vibrated. A low rumbling began.

Konstantine bellowed. "Do it!"

The optic feed went black, but not before the cat that had been scratching its chin on the sensor stalk backed away from the sensor.

And winked.

The audio feed still worked.

Ciarán wished it hadn't.

48

Ciarán settled into the drop module's crash seat and belted in. Maura Kavanagh plopped into the seat next to him.

She entwined her arm with his and squeezed. "Our first trip alone together without adult supervision. Whatever *will* we do?"

Ciarán jerked his chin toward the hatch.

Maura groaned. "Not that guy again."

Luther Gant cleared his throat and settled into the seat across from them. He belted in.

Helen Konstantine came aft to check on them. "I thought you two would go on to Unity Station on *Ibex*."

"Wing offered," Maura said, "but Ciarán is playing hard to get."

"I'm not. I just don't see Wing and Wisp getting along. Whereas Wisp loves Ship's Pilot Helen Konstantine."

"It's because I feed her."

Konstantine shouted at Luther Gant. "Hey, sourpuss!"

When he glared at her she tossed a ball of augustinite into his lap. "Play with the cat or feed it."

Maris Solon was single-handing to Contract system, and Ciarán dearly wanted to be there when she introduced herself to the Legion of Heroes. Sadly, he felt duty-bound to at least show up at Unity Station to be informed of his fate. He'd decided that it didn't matter, merchant license or not, he'd find something he could do aboard *Quite Possibly Alien* to keep busy.

"The prisoners?" Ciarán said.

"One in the autodoc forward," Konstantine said. "The rest locked in a drop module. All postmarked for the Dapper LT."

CIARÁN SLEPT most of the way to Sizemore. He didn't see Luther Gant debark, or Hector Poole take delivery of the prisoners.

Wisp, Maura, and Helen Konstantine departed on a direct route to Trinity Station and *Quite Possibly Alien*, traveling on a Kavanagh-flagged hull, one of the last Freeman vessels to leave Sizemore. The merchant guild hall had been mothballed and everything valuable loaded aboard, along with departing staff.

Maura commandeered a private stateroom for the trio, entirely sensible and entirely out of character. She was clearly rattled from her experience aboard *Ibex*. Normally Maura studiously avoided anything that indicated she was a Kavanagh daughter, one of several heirs to an enormous mercantile empire. When Ciarán offered to travel with them she laughed, and kicked him in the shin, an entirely Maura-like action, and one that put him at ease.

"We'll be fine," Maura said. "We won't open the hatch until we smell Will Gag's cooking."

"You might open a bit sooner," Ciarán said. "Say, upon docking at Trinity Station."

"The station has changed," Maura said. "It doesn't feel like home anymore."

"Maybe you've changed."

"I have. I'm even more awesome than I used to be." She kicked him again. "Aoife will send an escort. It's already arranged. Now jet, or you'll miss your connection."

"I am informed, Navigator."

"Good for you. Now move it before I do something we'll both enjoy."

49

Twelve days later Ciarán mac Diarmuid stood on Unity Station dock. He'd stopped counting the days since his scheduled interview with the Merchant Guild. He was toast, had to be, but he also had to go through the motions. Aoife nic Cartaí would interrogate him when she arrived. He remained her apprentice, and every insult or harm done by him would accrue to her as well. He had to see it through, not just for his own sake, but for hers, and for the crew's.

Unity Station was less than seventy years old, and it showed. Everything *worked*. There were no burned-out lamps on the hatch controls, no lifts that didn't, no out of order signs on the public toilets or vending kiosks. The station was half the size of Trinity Station but wasn't divided up into Freeman, League, and Ojin sectors. If he wanted to, he could circumnavigate the station without passing through a single security checkpoint or submit to a single customs inspection. It wasn't crowded either, and the scents wafting from the food carts and restaurants on the Arcade were familiar.

He didn't like anything about it. He was afraid to touch the lift call buttons for fear of smudging them. There wasn't a spot he could stand and watch the passers-by without feeling like he was on display. He wasn't a shadow-lurker, but there ought to be a place where no small number of the overhead luminaires were burned out or broken.

It felt like he was walking through a recorded drama set, one in which stylized *merchants extraordinary* returned from a trading mission to find that their spouse had invented a new type of macrofab, one that ran on perpetual motion and cranked out never-before-seen wonders, technology that would revolutionize the future and allow then to finally get that new apartment three tram stops closer to the Guild Hall. *And look, here are the keys to our new flitter. I'm having it waxed as we speak.*

The zero-radial tram *gleamed*. There wasn't a single fastener on it that looked like it had been scrounged off a burned-out longboat. His hullwalkers didn't stick to the deck plates, and no one tried to pick his pocket. They didn't look him in the eye, either, or move to make room when the tram grew crowded, or say please, or thank you, when he made room. At least that remained the same, else he'd have thought he'd been transported to some characterless purgatory, one where the lobby *and* the room looked exactly like the brochure. He wondered what it would feel like to be *from* Unity Station.

It would feel normal. Like being from Trinity Station felt to stationers. He was like a spindle rat getting his first glimpse of the Arcade.

Trinity Station was the Federation's spindle.

He'd thought it magnificent.

Unity Station was where serious people did serious business.

He knew he didn't belong here.

But he didn't belong on the planet, either.

Unity Surface was a nightmare compared to Trinity Surface. Barely habitable before the wreckage of the old station had pocked and gouged the northern hemisphere, the planet had never recovered. Unity Surface was a planet, barely. It had an economy, barely. And a population that *barely* outnumbered that of Trinity Surface's largest city by a hundred or more souls, at best.

Ciarán had felt, not smug or superior, but pleased, to say the least, hailing from the Federation's principal planet. If he ever met anyone from Unity Surface, he'd already decided to be magnanimous and effusive in his praise of their homeland in a generous celebration of their shared planetary heritage. Now he wasn't sure he could pull that off. If he ever found himself standing in downtown First Landing, chatting with a citizen, he wasn't certain he could refrain from pointing skyward, and asking the obvious questions. *What is wrong with you? Why aren't you up there?*

The Merchant Guild Hall stood across the arcade from the zero-radial tram. Beside it stood the towering edifice of the Stationmaster's Office. Together they spanned a broad arc, one fronted not by merchant stalls and mobile carts hawking wares, but by a wide green wedge of park with foliage and crisscrossed with winding pathways.

Ciarán gazed up at the Guild Hall entry. Perhaps a better pair of questions would be, *What is wrong with me? What am I doing here?*

Ciarán touched the hatch control. *What I'd promised.* The day he stopped doing that was the day they could plant him. That he hadn't know what he was getting into hadn't stopped him so far. At least no one was shooting at him.

Not yet, anyway.

He crossed the empty lobby to the check-in desk.

The Registry Boards hung overhead, listing all incoming and outgoing traffic for Unity Station and Trinity Station both. There were six large listing boards, and Unity Station traffic didn't fill the first one. The remaining five changed once, and of those five, one changed twice before all the Trinity Station traffic had been scrolled through. It wouldn't always be like that, every day, as there was a great deal of *going* from Trinity Station with the League pullout.

He scanned the boards for *Quite Possibly Alien*.

He hoped the war was short, and he expected it would be if the documents he'd reviewed were accurate. It seemed improbable that the League had started a war so they could kidnap Maura and him without starting a bigger war, but he'd lived through some crazy stuff, and that wouldn't be the craziest if true. Anyway, it wasn't Maura or him they were after but *Quite Possibly Alien*. And that made perfect sense. The drive technology the ship possessed was unique and impossible to value. And the threat its doomsday weapon posed was equally destabilizing.

An information and security desk sprawled beneath the boards. Large enough to seat a dozen but manned by a single soul, he marched up to the counter, his brain struggling to take in the sheer scope if it all, the shiny newness, the high ceilings, the hidden noise cancellation system that turned what should have been the echoing loneliness of a single pair of hullwalkers crossing hard deck to a solitary thump and a handful of subconscious clicks from the device in his pocket. *"Run!"* in the language of Contract System.

He placed his hand upon the tall counter and took a deep breath, inhaling absolutely nothing, the scent of Unity Station utterly devoid of character. He'd been there and back now, and every station had an odor, from the overcrowded reek of Ambidex, to the charred electronics miasma of Prescott Grange Station, unpleasant in the moment but certainly memorable and distinctly alive. He wondered if he reeked of days spent strapped in a crash seat, a jog half the length of Prix Canada's docking ring, and more days strapped down in steerage. It would be a miracle if he didn't pong like a sheepherder, and if he'd thought ahead, he might have taken a room, and cleaned up before marching into the Hall.

Every Guild Hall held transient quarters. He hadn't imagined he'd need to bathe before inquiring after a room for the night.

He glanced down at the attendant and laughed, the words torn from his lips before he could stop them. "Aren't you the colleen."

She grinned. "I am *sor*, and only nineteen years of age." She winked a stage wink.

A merchant apprentice like himself, she'd been abandoned to staff the vast lobby alone. Unlike him, she was red-haired and green-eyed, with alabaster skin and attired in fresh-pressed formals, an outfit he knew about but had never seen worn, being less spacer's utilities and more ethnic ceremonial garb. He half expected fiddles to start playing. If she stood and threw her shoulders back and burst into a bout of frenzied step dancing, he wouldn't blink an eye.

"How may I help you?"

The idea that he'd somehow walked onto a production set persisted.

"I'm after arriving," he said. "And seeking lodging fer the night. May I lay down by the fire, young miss?"

She consulted her workstation. "Let me ask my father, *sor*. He'd just out back in the cowshed."

Ciarán leaned on the counter but couldn't see the display. "Is he a sound sleeper, your father?"

"With a hobo vagabond in the house, and alone with his daughter?"

"With that."

"It's traditional," she said. "We can squeeze you in. Were you planning on smoking his pipe and wearing his slippers as well?"

"He owns *slippers*?"

They both laughed.

"Where you from?" she said.

And with that, he knew her. She wasn't asking where he'd just come from, or where he lived, or where he called home, but where he was *from*, from. Not just *him*, but his people. Everything else about him was transient. Was something he wore, like a suit of clothes, or a bad headache, or an education. Life could strip all of those away. Birth was destiny.

"You probably never heard of it."

She chuckled. "Try me."

"Oileán Chléire. It's—"

She seemed to gasp. "On Trinity Surface." Her face had become a placid mask. "You're the mac Diarmuid."

"Not me. That would be my father."

"That's not what I mean. You're the mac Diarmuid they're all up in arms about."

"I don't know who *they* are."

"*Everyone.* I need to call security."

"Don't do that. What's this about?"

"What isn't it about? You were supposed be here a fortnight ago—"

"I was detained."

"You should have rung up, then."

"It wasn't the sort of call-ahead detention."

"Said every *boyo*, ever."

"It's true. Now who is it—"

"I'm calling security. I don't want whatever's coating you to rub off on me."

"Just point me toward your supervisor, then."

"I would have already, but it's the middle of the middle of the night!"

"It's the start of first shift," Ciarán said. "I checked."

"It's the start of first shift on *Trinity Station*. We're one-eighty out on account of the station fall."

"I don't understand."

"Our clocks and the Trinity Station clocks are off by half a day. It's so that if there's ever another emergency there will be a first-shift stationmaster available, so long as the superluminal nodes stay up."

"I never heard of that."

"If you'd rung up you would have. It's new. It started with the war."

"I—"

"It's a royal pain," she said. "They could have shifted the clocks on Trinity Station but no, they're too *high and mighty* for that. I'm junior and I'm out here by myself, while all my friends are on first and second shifts, and you're to blame. I'm calling security."

"Don't do that. And how am I to blame? I'm not the Trinity Station authorities."

"I never said you were. You're to blame because you started the war."

"I didn't."

"That's not what I hear."

"Who is saying that?"

"I told you already. *Everyone.*" She glanced up at him. "Security's not answering." She pointed deeper into the building. "Go wait at the bar."

"The bar?"

"Or in the lounge, take your pick. Get on with you."

"I will." There would be someone at the bar or in the lounge that could fill a stranger in on what sort of trouble this mac Diarmuid fellow might find himself in.

"I told you to go."

Ciarán nodded. "You did." There existed a form to these meetings. A societal expectation. It was beyond rude to ignore the shape of first meetings, unless he'd been declared dead, or an outcast.

"Kate," she said. "Kate O'Neill. From Slane town."

"On Unity Surface?"

"Why else would I be on third shift, and the rest of them in their sleeping?"

"Jealousy," Ciarán said. "I imagine you're either the prettiest or the cleverest of your cohort."

"Why can't I be both?"

"I wouldn't bet against you so being."

A shadow of a smile flashed across her face. "There's two men looking for you. They're in the lounge."

"Or at the bar."

"Aye."

"When did they arrive?"

"A fortnight ago."

"And they're yet waiting."

"Aye. But they don't seem happy about it."

"Neither am I."

"Then we're all in agreement." She put one hand on her hip and pointed with the other. "Now get on with you, you night slinker."

Ciarán hitched his bug-out bag higher on his shoulders. "I will. Fair play to you, Kate Ui Néill, and thanks for the warning."

"Like your lot need it," she said. "Tell Mr. Moore's shadow his package has arrived. It's like a matchmaker's convention around here, I swear."

Ciarán swallowed. "Gilpatrick Moore? Truxton's fixer?"

"And his shadow. Tell them, the package, and if there's going to be bloodshed, kindly take it outside."

50

T he barroom and the lounge were attached, the bar itself and a narrow hallway dividing the two compart- ments, the design similar to pubs at home and on Trinity Station. Ciarán's brother Mícheál owned a pub in Black- pool, on the mainland, and it shared the same general layout but without the fine finishes and ornamental touches. It was as if someone had decided to build a shrine to public houses, and had spared no expense. The place seemed deserted but for the barman and a pair of customers, one sitting at the bar, and the other holding down a table in the lounge. When he entered they both stood and began heading in his direction. A footie game was playing on a viewscreen mounted above the bar sandwiched between the scrolling inbound and outbound Registry displays.

Ciarán shucked out of his backpack and took a seat at one of the barroom tables. He sat facing the entry in case the colleen had actually called security.

Gilpatrick Moore was a small dark man, with bones and smoldering punks woven into his dreadlocked hair. He stood beside Ciarán, his hands stuffed in the pockets of a merchant captain's greatcoat, though one lined in yellow instead of the traditional red. Moore and Truxton were inseparable in Ciarán's mind, both being fixtures on Trinity Station and living legends. People said Gilpatrick Moore had been a priest ages ago, but he was a hundred if he was a day, and his dead long past waking, even if it mattered, which it didn't. He was Truxton's matchmaker, and trouble of the first water. That he'd been cooling his heels, waiting for Ciarán for two weeks didn't bode well.

Ciarán remained seated, and Moore stood, but it didn't put a pain in Ciarán's neck to look him in the eye. "Did the Stationmaster send you or Truxton?" It seemed a lifetime ago that Ciarán had killed a Truxton merchant, but then he didn't have the luxury of time and distance to consider the fallout. That Merchant Roche was a slaver and a tool of Ixatl-Nine-Go might not yet be common knowledge.

Moore had a whispery voice, one that required concentration to hear. "You're in my seat."

Ciarán stood. He towered over Moore, which would be a good thing in a fistfight, with his superior reach, but men like Gilpatrick Moore didn't brawl.

Ciarán smiled, surprised at his own thoughts. "Suit yourself."

Men like Ciarán mac Diarmuid didn't brawl either. He wondered when he'd become that man, and when it had started to show.

He took the seat to Moore's left, moving his chair closer to Moore before he sat. He'd heard the man was left-handed. If he wanted to draw down on Ciarán he'd find it hard to do without risking a snapped wrist, if Ciarán remained alert and on the ball.

Which was made decidedly harder when the second man took the seat to Ciarán's left.

"One expects a merchant apprentice to hew to a schedule, my good man."

Ciarán glanced at Hector Poole.

"I was detained."

"Indeed. Well, you're here now. Shall we begin?"

Ciarán planted his feet. He shifted his chair. "Begin what?"

Gilpatrick Moore had a wheezy laugh. "He'll do."

"I told you he would," Hector Poole said. "You need only read his file to—"

"And I told you. Everything I need to know about a man—"

Poole waved his hand airily. "Spare me the Freeman bromide. I can't possibly see how you can judge a man's usefulness by how he enters a room and takes a seat."

"He also talked," Moore said.

"Fourteen words," Poole said. "He has spoken fourteen words in your presence."

"I knew after nine." Moore dipped his left hand into his pocket. He glanced at Ciarán's fingers swaddling his wrist. When he looked Ciarán in the eye he smiled. "Stationmaster's compliments."

Ciarán released his grip and Moore deposited a data crystal on the table.

"What is it?" Poole said.

"My personnel records," Ciarán said. "Everything the Academy and Trinity Station authorities have on me. I am led to believe the contents are... damning."

Poole glanced at Gilpatrick Moore. "Are they?"

"He doesn't know," Ciarán said. "He hasn't looked."

"I doubt that is—"

Moore shifted in his seat.

"Material, shall we say? Your assessment of the contents, merchant apprentice?"

"They're either damning," Ciarán said. "Or they're a lie."

"Show me," Moore said.

Ciarán removed the chain of pendant spires from his backpack. When he placed them on the table Moore grunted and turned away.

"*Tinker's Dam*," he said. "Who did this?"

"A Huangxu Eng death camp commandant. He confessed to Ship's Captain Danny Swan."

"The matches braided into your hair," Poole said. "How do you keep them lit?"

"They're not matches," Moore said.

"They're slow burning fuses." Ciarán recognized them from home. He glanced at Hector Poole. "You've been here together for two weeks, and this is the first time you thought to ask that?"

"We're not here together. We couldn't be more separate in our aims."

"Which are?"

"Mr. Moore would like you to take a Truxton commission and hunt down the Outsider you've let loose. I, on the other hand, want you to do something dangerous and possibly fatal."

"And that is?"

"I haven't decided yet. Shall we turn on the news, and see what game remains afoot?"

"Let's not," Moore said.

Hector Poole leaned forward in his seat, his hands hidden beneath the table. When he grinned the wolf behind his eyes stared out. "Let's."

"Barman," Moore shouted. "Change the damned channel."

51

"I t appears there is very much yet unsettled in the world," Hector Poole said.

The regular news had been preempted by a special report bulletin, which seemed to be the case every time Ciarán turned the news on, which was never unless he was expected to do so for work.

There was no profit in anything that made it to the news channels. The broadcast news was like a periscope zoomed in on yesterday's opportunities, triumphs that he felt stupid for missing out on, or disasters that he felt lucky to have avoided. There was no guidance for what he should do tomorrow unless he wanted to run with the herd, which never worked out for people like him, natural born stragglers easily picked off and preyed upon. The only people who profited in that situation where the other stragglers kicking up dust right in front of him.

There'd been a mass murder in Sizemore space. Thirty-six people dead and several yet unaccounted for. A culturally attractive newsreader stood in front of a display screen speaking in somber erlspout about the tragedy, a horrible nightmare made even more tragic because the murderer wasn't one of their own, but a Freeman.

A Freeman who had escaped on a salvaged League super-luminal.

It felt like someone had kicked him in the guts. "I didn't do that," Ciarán said.

"How could you?" Moore said. "It's a real time feed coming in over the superluminal node."

"Oh, right," Ciarán said, but he didn't feel much better. "That's not going to help end the war."

"There you are wrong," Poole said. "That war is over. Now pipe down and pay attention."

There had been a prisoner exchange arranged, one between the Hundred Planets and the League. One senior Eng official for twenty-four low-level League captives, the exchange to take place on one of Sizemore's uninhabited moons. Apparently the League had a specially constructed prisoner exchange facility on the fourth planet's tertiary moon, a blocky building that reminded Ciarán of the emergency survival shelters in Prescott Grange space.

They had a visual-only recording of the murders, which they would run after the commercial break.

"That's ghoulish," Ciarán said.

"It's Erlish," Moore said. "The Four Bs. Bullets, Blood,—"

"My mother was not unmarried," Poole said. "And she was not a dog. Nearly everyone in the League can say the same."

"And they can say it with minty fresh breath," Ciarán said. The broadcasters were running an advert for mouthwash as intro to their snuff film.

Moore chuckled.

Hector Poole did not.

"I nearly forgot," Ciarán said. "The colleen at the front desk says your package has arrived."

"Good," Poole said, pointing at the display. "Now watch carefully."

There were two parties of four. They faced each other from across a compartment. Ten meters separated them. The exchange had been recorded from a point midway between the parties, at deckhead height. He could tell they were ten meters apart because a graduated scale had been projected below the scene. The recording was wide angle, with very little detail. It almost looked staged, so grainy was the feed.

One in each party stood handcuffed and hooded. The commentator stated that the hooded League captive was a Lieutenant Commander Manson, missing in action and presumed dead for nearly twenty years. There were twenty-three additional League captives being delivered aboard an inbound freighter. The Huangxu Eng captive, Admiral Shi Quin Fan, a senior administrator in the Hundred Planets.

"He's a death camp commander and a war criminal," Ciarán said.

"Only according to those who know him," Poole said. "Don't listen. Just watch."

It was impossible not to listen. It was as if the commentator were announcing a sports game.

"Is that the *Tinker's Dam* murderer?" Moore said.

"It is," Ciarán said. He'd been wearing the chain of *Thinker's Dame* pendant spires when Ciarán had darted him in the eye.

They pulled the hoods off and it was definitely Shi. He looked the same, smug and superior, except he was wearing a black eyepatch.

Lieutenant Commander Manson didn't look like he'd been missing for twenty years. It hadn't been a fortnight since Ciarán had seen him on a troop shuttle bound for Sizemore.

"I thought he was dead," Moore said.

Luther Gant didn't look dead. He looked... vengeful. Ciarán

had known the man all his life and not once could he recall seeing him wear the spire.

The three Huangxu Eng escorts moved swiftly, bang sticks striking out, dropping the three League guards to the deck in an instant. They turned to face the optical sensor, and like a precision drill team, ejected the power supplies from what were now obviously not bang sticks, but Huangxu-style stunners.

Admiral Shi said something. The woman, who was most certainly Wing Zixin, said something, and then the three of them left the compartment.

Luther Gant removed his hands from behind his back. He rubbed his wrists and dropped the handcuffs to the deck.

He reached into his pocket and pulled out gloves.

Correction. Not gloves. *Hardhands.*

"I've seen enough," Ciarán said.

"I haven't," Moore said.

"I'll watch it again," Poole said. "Though I doubt I'll enjoy it any more than the first time."

Ciarán dug in his bug-out bag.

His Hardhands were missing.

"I believe it's rather cunning of the man," Poole said.

"Honest, your honor," Moore said. "I didn't lay a hand on him."

They both laughed.

Luther Gant quite literally disarmed Admiral Shi and the man yet lived.

Gant wasn't quite done with Shi's dismembering.

Both of them flinched, Ciarán with them.

"Ouch," Poole said.

Ciarán glanced away from the display. "There is nothing funny about this."

"No, there isn't," Poole said. "No one in the Hundred Planets will be laughing when they witness this humiliation at the hands of a Freeman. Nor will they laugh when League evidence of Shi's atrocities going back decades is accidentally leaked, or the subsequent results of the Reynard's investigation into the disappearance of the *Thinker's Dame* are published."

"Seamus is looking into that?"

"Can you think of anyone better for the job?"

"I can't."

"And Luther Gant?"

"We'll release him, of course. Might even give him a medal on the sly. He didn't attack our people. That was the Mighty Eighty-Eight, who, against all odds, penetrated League defenses, unaided, and delivered justice to a renegade thug. Shi proved an embarrassment to the empire, and he was dealt with by agents of the empire, with an assist from their ancient enemy. Publicly."

"We are one," Moore said.

"Indeed," Hector Poole said. "If you check you will find that Luther Gant filed intent against Shi for the defilement and murder of his wife, supported by the sworn testimony of Ship's Captain Danny Swan, whom Shi confessed to. Shi also confessed to the defilement and torture of League prisoners."

"Including your wife," Ciarán said.

"Ex-wife." Poole gazed at the screen. "She jettisoned me long ago."

"So I'll have Luther Gant as a neighbor again."

"Hardly," Poole said. "It appears Maris made a side arrangement with Luther Gant, offering him a lift out of the system in exchange for his title."

"Title to what?" Moore said. "He's officially dead."

"Maris Solon is now the Solon of Clear Island, on paper at least. If there's an extended court battle—"

"There won't be," Moore said. "Macer Gant is gone and won't be coming back."

"There's the two boys," Ciarán said. "Macer's step-brothers."

"There were," Poole said. "They've gone missing. Run away the orphanage says, but—"

"Murdered by the other brats," Moore said.

"Or the staff," Poole said. "The so-called Gant children proved to be...destructively sociopathic. The airlock logs are complete but inconclusive as to the identity of the operator that... dealt with them."

"Someone spaced two children," Ciarán said.

"Two murderous monsters," Poole said. "If one believes the orphanage records."

"You've been busy," Moore said.

"I've been exhaustive. I hate loose ends."

Something flashed on the news channel display. They were still running the Sizemore mass murder story.

"Templeman drive failure," Poole said. "On the prisoner exchange vessel."

The newsreader said that the Hundred Planets had delivered the exchange prisoners aboard a captured Q-ship, a clandestine superluminal disguised as an in-system freighter. When it became clear that the exchange wouldn't happen, they turned and boosted toward the tripwire.

The League vessel intending to receive the prisoners attempted to intervene. The loss was positively devastating to the League. The Commandant of the Naval Academy had been in command of the receiving vessel. Admiral Steyr's daughter, Warrant Officer Omega Steyr, was amongst the prisoners to be exchanged, as were nearly two dozen Academy cadets captured while on a training exercise. Shortly after Steyr attempted a forced boarding the mag bottle breached.

"The prisoners from Persephone," Ciarán said. "You had them killed."

"I did not *have them killed*," Poole said. "I killed them, as surely as if I'd pressed a nerve disruptor to their foreheads and pulled the trigger. They were chemically interrogated and there was no doubt. They were not children, being used. They were willing participants in a clandestine plot against the League and, if not our allies, at least our neighbors. It is our Queen's opinion, and thus the League's policy, that *Quite Possibly Alien* is a sentient being, a League citizen, and thus entitled to life, liberty, and the unqualified protection of a just and benevolent sovereign. I acted in accordance with Her Highness's wishes and in full compliance with our laws and traditions."

"In secret," Moore said. "Without trial."

"They were guilty as sin. There would have been no trial."

"Because they're above the law."

"Because their families believe they are the law." Poole tapped his fingertip twice against the tabletop. "They are mistaken."

Poole turned to Ciarán. "In a moment Mr. Moore will offer you an opportunity. Become a merchant. A Truxton captain, with your own vessel and crew. Go hunt down this Outsider you've released. Hunt it down and kill it."

"It wore the spire," Ciarán said.

"It strapped a table leg to its head," Moore said. "Aping its captors."

"I don't believe that," Ciarán said.

"Then you only need to find it," Moore said. "And tell me where it is."

"And your offer?" Ciarán said.

"I'd like you to follow the truth," Poole said. "Follow it as I have. Wherever it leads you."

"And if I find it?"

"When you do." He glanced at his hands. "Set it free."

"How would I do that?"

"By throwing everything away. The career you wanted. The life you imagined. Your family. Your friends. The woman you love. The respect of your peers. Chuck it all."

"What were you, before you became this... man you are now?"

"A history professor."

"And then what happened?"

"I met Manus Manusson. And later, Lionel Aster. Lord Aster, as you know him. And I began to question... everything."

"You want me to become a murderer and a spy, like you."

"I'd like you to chart your own course. I doubt you'd make the choices I made."

"Then what?"

"Whatever you like. The situation in the Federation and in the League will continue to devolve. There will be additional attempts to capture or kill *Quite Possibly Alien* and at least some of its crew. You and yours should clear out, get far away, and allow the dust to settle. Aren't you the least bit interested about Kirill Olek and where he came from?"

"I know where he came from."

Poole stared at Ciarán.

Ciarán stared back. "When we first met. Was it a coincidence?"

"I thought at first it was," Poole said. "You look nothing like your mother. Not even your eyes. It was like she was gone and had never lived. I checked on your brothers. They have her look. But they are nothing like her.

"I imagined she was lost, along with the *Willow Bride*. When I found her death book in your kit—"

"You chattered."

"I had to. I didn't know what else to do. The iron rule—"

"There are no good coincidences."

"Exactly. No joy would come of our meeting. Just as no joy had come from my meeting Lionel Aster, all those years before."

"My mother. What was she like? As a girl."

"Utterly fearless."

"And?"

"And that's it," Poole said. "There was nothing else special about her. There didn't need to be.

"That she had married a farmer seemed ridiculous to me. That she had an aspiring merchant for a son seemed even more absurd."

"Because?"

"Because she was a warrior. Once she knew her heart the price didn't matter."

"Are you Charles Newton?"

"There is no Charles Newton, and there hasn't been for a very long time. He's an invention of convenience. Manusson needed a front man. Three of us took turns being Charles Newton once the real Charles Newton died in combat. We'd lost the war, but we hadn't lost everything. Then the *Widow Bride* and Manusson disappeared, and with them all hope.

"We couldn't search for the lost ship and crew. Not without being caught and executed. So we decided to hide and time travel. Taking turns in cryo. One of us waking up, every year at first, alternately, then every five years, then ten, then fifty, always waking long enough to scour the feeds for news of Manusson, your mother, and the *Willow Bride*. After a couple hundred years the risk of being executed had disappeared but the thought of staying awake wasn't that appealing. Those were dark days, in a dark age.

"About a thousand years ago the League became livable again but we both agreed to carry on time traveling. The League was spreading out, and maybe they'd uncover something during the expansion.

"Thirty years ago, my counterpart woke me. She'd found a clue. We've both been largely active since then."

"You and Anastasia Blum."

"Right."

"And you're not a descendant of my uncle. You're my actual uncle. My mother's brother."

"Right."

"And you want me to give up everything, steal *Quite Possibly Alien* from my mentor and hare off to Earth. To look for quicksilver aliens."

"I doubt you'd have to steal *Quite Possibly Alien*. And I don't want you to do it. But I think you should."

"Why?"

"Because it's what she would have done." Hector Poole stood. "Think it over. Regardless of what you decide I'm glad I met you, Ciarán mac Diarmuid. Even if it truly was a coincidence."

"Is that it?" Ciarán said. "Your entire pitch?"

"I think it is. Now I have a package to retrieve. Good luck with your examination."

Ciarán watched him go. What he'd just said was hard to digest all at once. Later they'd sit down and he could really dig in. After he'd thought it all over and had time to come up with proper questions. There was so much he wanted to know.

He turned to speak to Gilpatrick Moore. The smaller man leapt upon him, he was on the deck, Moore on top of him, as a fireball burst through the open hatch and the barroom glassware all exploded at once.

52

They stumbled through the hatch and into the arms of an emergency response team. The emergency crew hustled them out of the Guild Hall lobby and into an emergency stairwell. No one would tell Ciarán anything, and no one asked him anything either. The barman, Gilpatrick Moore, and he had superficial injuries only, so the lot of them were shuffled up the stairwell in the rear and parked in an employee break room a deck above. When that began to grow crowded as first-shift workers arrived, they were shifted five decks higher to a visitor's waiting room outside the guild master's office. There were chairs around the periphery of the compartment, a couple tables with table lamps, and a low table before a couch with a number of brochures about the delights of Unity Station scattered about on it. They sat in a trio of chairs near the guild master's office entry.

An hour later they were still sitting there when the barman glanced at his handheld and said, "That's it, I'm off shift," and walked out.

He might have been picked up for a statement on his way out, or he might have evaded their captors entirely.

The pair of them sat there a while longer before anyone spoke.

"You don't seem very broken up," Moore said.

"About?"

"Your uncle being blown to bits."

"I didn't know he was my uncle until he said. I'd only suspected we might be related on account of his name and my mother's. And I've been thinking about all he said, and how being my uncle seems to be the least important part of it."

"A man you know then," Moore said.

"Being blown to bits? I'm not sure that happened. I've decided not to form an opinion until I know if the colleen was also blown to bits."

"The new girl at the reception desk?"

"That's right. I've been fooled twice now by Luther Gant. Without a body to look at I'm not making up my mind. And even with a body, it might be a hound."

"You can't make a hound but from a dead man," Moore said.

"You'd think that, but you'd be wrong. You can't make a hound without killing a man's body. That doesn't mean you've killed the man."

"That's news," Moore said.

"I think," Ciarán said, "That I am now in possession of so much news that I could charge anything I wanted for it, up to and including a merchant captain's greatcoat and a superluminal."

"To use or to own?"

"To own."

"That would be hard to ascertain before the fact."

"I wouldn't want it then. I'd want it afterwards. All I'd need up front is the word of a trustworthy man."

"Those are rare."

"I know a fair number."

Moore nodded. "You're turning down my offer, I take it."

"To hunt and kill the Outsider? I won't do it. You'd think it was an animal, to look at it, or some sort of bug, but it was wearing the spire, and it understood Adderly when she spoke to it."

"Adderly?"

"One of its kin, in a way."

"There's more than one of them?"

"Outsiders? Not that I know of. But they'd been breeding it, trying to make a version of an Outsider they could control."

"I don't believe that," Moore said. "No one would be so stupid."

"If you say so." Ciarán stretched his legs out. They weren't going to tell them anything and they weren't going to let them go. It was the way of the world. He could see that now.

He'd been naive in his understanding of power, largely because he'd never wanted any. And now that he had some, for knowledge truly is power, he couldn't just hand it away. He wanted to be taken seriously, and listened to, and the best way to do that was to put a high value on what he knew that others didn't so that they'd feel they had to consider what he had to say seriously, or else admit they'd been duped by a merchant apprentice.

"Supposing I knew one. An honest man. When would you be wanting the superluminal?"

"I don't want a superluminal for myself," Ciarán said. "I want one as a gift. For a friend."

"Macer Gant."

"What I know is worth at least as much as the loan balance on *Tractor Four Squared*."

"I could do the merchant captain's license or the superluminal. But not both. Take your pick."

"The superluminal." He'd only asked for the license so that there would be something he could bargain away.

"Fair enough," Moore said. "How much longer do you reckon we should sit here?"

"I have to stick because I need to talk to the guild master."

"Slip a note under her door and come on."

"I'm in enough trouble as it is. Squirt me your id addy and I'll call you when someone shows up."

"Fine," Moore said.

"Do we have a deal?" Ciarán said.

"I'll talk to Truxton."

"Oh, well, in that case I'll also want a core dump on everything he knows that I don't already know. Sort of a two-way conversation."

"You can't just arbitrarily change the deal."

"You're the one changed it. You didn't mention you were looping in third parties." Ciarán grinned. "I'll trust the merchant captain to be forthcoming, should we agree."

Moore glared at him, nodding slowly to himself. "People underestimate you."

"I guess that's better than them overestimating me, and my leaving them disappointed."

"It's a more dangerous way to live."

"I wouldn't know."

Moore stared at him. He scratched his chin. He leaned forward, elbows on his knees. He whispered in his already whispery voice. "What are you going to do, if there's a body?"

"He might be my uncle," Ciarán said. "But he hadn't taken the Oath."

"So, no matchmaking on his account."

"You're the expert. I don't think it would fit with custom."

"It wouldn't fit with Freeman custom." Moore's gaze met his. "But before we were Freemen?"

"We were sons and daughters," Ciarán said. "The thought has occurred."

"Do not make a move on this station without first consulting me," Moore said. "Is that clear?"

Ciarán nodded. "As crystal."

Moore held out his hand.

Ciarán blinked. "Whose hand am I shaking? Truxton's man's, or Truxton's?"

"Neither," Moore said. "That before you be the hand of a brother."

Ciarán gripped Moore's hand and pulled him to his feet.

"Wait here," Moore said.

Four hours later the guild master breezed into the compartment, a pair of assistants in tow.

Ciarán rose as she approached.

She glanced at him and scowled. "Tomorrow, at ten. Don't be late again."

"Wait," Ciarán said. He handed her a data crystal.

"What's this?" She tossed the crystal to one of her aides.

"My personnel files from the Academy and the Trinity Station stationmaster."

"I asked for those a fortnight ago."

"I'd heard that."

"Did you tamper with them?"

"I haven't even looked at them."

"And you don't think I should look at them either."

"That's not for me to say."

"That's right. It isn't." She thumbed the lock on her office hatch and the trio disappeared inside.

Ciarán messaged Gilpatrick Moore, who sent him the hatch code for a private hostel compartment on the third deck of the guild hall. He instructed Ciarán to lock himself in until his merchant's examination tomorrow morning.

"Food," Ciarán messaged. He hadn't had anything to eat since docking and his tubed ration supply was running low. Not to mention even the best meal pastes were disgusting. He'd been looking forward to some actual human food.

"In the room," Moore replied.

The lifts were working again but Ciarán headed for the stairwell. There was a great deal of scurrying about going on, whether emergency workers, investigators, or regular business, he couldn't tell. He took the stairs, wary of the lift and its potential for unwanted company.

He found the hostel wing on the third deck, no problem, and the specified compartment, a defensible position at the end of the hallway adjacent to the stairwell. Moore had him spooked, and he found himself thinking like a fugitive, which he wasn't, unless he was and just didn't know it yet. Either way, it was good practice, being careful. He imagined Moore had taken the compartment directly across the corridor as well. It wouldn't do to step into the corridor just as the hatch opposite opened to reveal an enemy.

Ciarán glanced both ways before trying the lock.

It was the right compartment.

He eased inside and shucked his bug-out bag off his shoulders.

He flicked the lights on and groaned. There was a stack of Huangxu tubed rations on his worktable and a woman, bound and gagged, stretched out on his bunk.

He took a seat in the workstation chair and messaged Moore. "The body?"

"Vaporized, I hear," Moore messaged. "Open at nine sharp. No earlier. Best get some rack time."

Ciarán pressed his palms against his forehead. He let his breath out slowly.

His hands were shaking. He hadn't realized how keyed up he'd been, how angry... sad... outraged... he wasn't sure which, at the idea of Hector Poole being dead and gone. He'd only met the man twice, but he felt he knew him after his conversations with Konstantine and Maris Solon. And nearly every aspect of his life since he'd met Poole had been guided by Poole's invisible hand. He'd been used and manipulated. Forced into situations that would have killed a weaker man—or driven him mad. And all because of a chance meeting with his two-thousand-year-old uncle. If there was an event less likely to occur in a man's life, he couldn't think of one. Unless it was digging up a two-thousand-year-old woman in a neighbor's barley field and marrying her.

There were no good coincidences. That was what the iron law said. So if he and Hector Poole had met by coincidence then that meant that the fallout from the meeting wouldn't turn out well for either of them. But if it hadn't been coincidence, but the result of some hidden hand, that would be even worse, particularly for a puppet master like Poole. It meant someone was pulling his strings.

Ciarán scooted his chair next to the bunk. A handwritten note rested on Kate Ui Néill's bodice. She glared at him when he picked it up and read it. The first line was printed in League script and underlined. Twice.

I have been a naughty girl.

Under that was written a single sentence, in a different hand, and in Freeman text. Written repeatedly down the page. What looked like a hundred times, at least.

I will not interfere with the post or attempt to read another's mail.

Ciarán chuckled and loosened her gag. "Would you like me to untie you?"

She looked him up and down.

"Well?"

"I'm thinking about it."

"Let me know when you make your mind up."

"I have. You can untie me. But don't harm the ties."

"Because?"

"Because you might want to tie me up later."

"Why would I want to do that?"

"Because I asked you to." She wriggled against her restraints. She held her bound hands outstretched before her. "But first let's have some dinner and see where things lead from there."

53

A t nine sharp Ciarán opened the hostel stateroom hatch and yawned.

Gilpatrick Moore glared at his from the open hatch across the corridor. "Good way to get yourself killed."

Kate Ui Néill kissed Ciarán's cheek and strode off along the corridor. "You can keep the ties."

"I'll do that," Ciarán said. He might want to hang himself later.

Moore watched her go. "Good way to get yourself murdered, messing with the stationmaster's daughter."

"She's the stationmaster's daughter? She told me she was from the planet. Slane town."

"Slain, not Slane. That's what they call the crater where the bulk of the old station landed."

"Oh. Well, nothing happened."

Moore snorted. "Around you? I don't believe that's possible."

"It's true." He'd slept in the workstation chair, and had the backache to prove it.

"Sure it is. Let's see you. Step out."

Ciarán dressed in his dark blue *Quite Possibly Alien* utilities. They had his name and his vessel's name on them, but he hadn't had time to attach any of the spacer's badges marking the ports he'd visited. He hadn't even brought the only ones he had, from Ambidex and Prescott Grange, the beginning and end of his apprentice cruise.

"That'll do. We'll break our fast at the canteen and then up you go to the auditorium."

"I'll try not to soil my clothes with nutrient paste."

"You could be spotless as a saint and they're not going to give you a merchant's license. But at least you'll get a good last meal as a merchant apprentice."

"They might give me a license." That, or let him keep his apprentice ticket. There was always a chance.

"And I might pay for breakfast." Moore opened the stairwell hatch. "Come on with you, apprentice purser."

Three decks down they exited into the lobby. A tall merchant captain in a freshly pressed greatcoat stood, hands on hips, surveying the wreckage of the Guild Hall lobby. He had a fresh haircut. He stroked his sharply trimmed ginger beard like it was a new idea, one he wasn't certain about yet. He turned at the sound of Moore's steps and grinned. "Looks like a bomb went off in here."

"It does look it," Moore said. "Merchant Captain Ruairí Kavanagh, meet Merchant Apprentice Ciarán mac Diarmuid. Ciarán is buying us a meal."

Kavanagh nodded. "Seeking to buy my vote, Merchant Apprentice?"

Ciarán felt his face heat. "I—"

"It's Ruairí's first examination as a merchant captain," Moore said. "He doesn't get a vote."

"Only merchants vote on merchant licenses," Kavanagh said. "There's nothing improper, Merchant Apprentice. I made a poor joke and now regret it."

"I should have known that," Ciarán said.

"You can't know everything," Kavanagh said. "But I hope you know where the canteen is."

"He doesn't," Moore said. "But he knows a guy."

SOMEHOW CIARÁN ENDED up buying breakfast for a score of ship's captains and merchant captains, maybe more. It seemed that every Truxton and Kavanagh merchant captain knew Gilpatrick Moore by sight, which wasn't surprising given his dreadlocks and smoldering punks, and about half the nic Cartaí captains knew him as well. They were forced to eject a brace of merchant apprentices from a large round table in the center of the canteen, one where the Registry boards could be read from every seat.

"Here she comes." A nic Cartaí ship's captain pointed at the outbound boards.

"Good," Ruairí Kavanagh said. "She took my advice."

"Who did?" Ciarán asked.

"Your master," Kavanagh said. "Aoife nic Cartaí."

"What advice?"

"The new name for her vessel. She wanted to call it, *The Thin Stars*, which would never have worked, since it wouldn't show up on the boards like that, but in some truncated form."

"She's renamed *Quite Possibly Alien*?"

"That old hulk? You can't even get a dozen cans on its mast, and those you have to manhandle on and off in hardsuits. I'm speaking of *Golden Parachute*, or rather, *Thin Star*, as it's now registered."

"I thought that wreck would never leave the dock," a nic Cartaí captain said. "The yard's been backed up for nearly a year thanks to whoever the idiot was who lit up a longboat's main drive *inside the boat bay*."

"They should make whoever did that pay for the damage," someone said. "And for our time and lost profits, waiting in queue."

Ruairí Kavanagh stroked his beard. "They should at least make him pay for breakfast."

"Senior captain on deck," someone shouted.

The Truxton captains lurched to their feet as one.

Gilpatrick Moore kept his seat. He nodded at Ciarán, and when he stood Ciarán stood.

Ship's Captain Danny Swan leaned on a cane. The woman at his side leaned on him.

Swan shook hand after hand as he crossed the room. He looked... not recovered, but recovering. Anastasia Blum appeared physically well but seemed to flinch at every loud voice, her gaze darting from face to face.

When her gaze met Ciarán's it froze. She blushed and turned away.

Somehow Ciarán had crossed the compartment. He stood before her. He took her hand.

"Merchant, forgive me. Would you like to sit?"

"I would," she said, and he led her apart from the others to a table near the hatch. She seemed to breathe a little easier.

"Ciarán—"

"Do not wake the dead, I beg you." He took her hand and pursued her gaze until she had no choice but to meet his. "All is forgotten."

"Not all," she said. "I won't allow it."

"I hadn't expected to see you here."

"When I met you, I thought you might prove a competent merchant."

"I think I might yet. They could still grant me a merchant license."

She squeezed his hand. "That won't happen. Mine will be the only vote cast in your favor."

"Others might be persuaded. If I make a good showing at the examination."

"You won't. Because you aren't a competent merchant. I wanted to see you, before the meeting. To tell you that."

"I see."

"It is said that in ancient times, when men plied the seas instead of the stars, that cities would build lighthouses to guide their mariners safely to port. One such city built a giant statue of a man straddling the opening of their harbor, holding a lantern to guide the way. Many mariners were guided by that light. Many merchants.

"When Vatya rode me, and we first laid eyes on you..." A tear rolled down her cheek. "She trembled."

"Please," Ciarán said. "Stop."

Annie swallowed. "We both trembled."

"Merchant—"

"I must do this, Ciarán. I must."

"Why?"

"Because you need to know. I *lived* everything she did. I *felt* everything she felt." Her face had grown crimson.

She turned away. "I *saw* you. I saw you as *she* saw you."

"Annie—"

"The darkness does not fear merchants, Ciarán." She licked her lips. "But it trembles before the light, and the colossus that bears it."

"I'm not—"

"You are. I knew then, in that instant, that Vatya would lose, that even if it cost my life, there would be nothing for her but failure. She knew it as well, as she had access to my memories. She was aware of the *Willow Bride* and Manusson's project because I was aware. I was part of the experiment from the beginning. That's why Vatya sent Olek to Clear Island. To find Manusson's work, to root it out, and to end it.

"She thought, because *I* thought, that you were not ready,

that you had taken the reins and raced ahead of the field, alone, defiant, and unprepared. You'd signed with pirates to escape your mundane existence."

"They're not pirates."

"I know that. But they might well have turned pirate without you. Aoife is strong willed and impulsive. She needed a sea anchor to keep her off the rocks. Someone to steady her while she took in sail and found her course. The woman you know is not the woman I hired immediately after the Murrisk incident.

"You saved her. Just as you saved me."

"You give me credit I don't deserve."

"Allow me my illusions, then." She laced her fingers together and sighed. "There are days when I consider taking my own life. When the weight of what I've done... as Vatya's mount, as a woman fleeing her own mortality, as a flawed and imperfect vessel soiled beyond redemption.

"One thought alone stays my hand. The thought of Ciarán mac Diarmuid. What might his future hold? What wonders will he discover? What bright future will his children build?

"I will vote for you, as merchant, and then I will sleep. A hundred years, a thousand, I've not yet decided. Whatever I choose, when I wake..."

"When you do, Merchant?"

She looked him in the eye. "I will expect marvels, Ciarán. Marvels."

54

At ten on the dot Ciarán arrived for his merchant examination. The room chosen was the third largest in the Guild Hall, one used for administrative hearings and arbitrations.

A high bench, with seating for a devil's dozen, had seven places set for use, each with a name placard.

In front of that by a meter or so, and a meter lower in height, stood a simple table and a single chair, what they called the pleading table. The room could be set up with a pair of pleading tables, so it appeared there wasn't any arbitration scheduled for later, or any in-person evidence offered, either for or against him.

Behind that, separated by two meters or so, stood a rail, and behind that what they called the gallery, general seating for people involved with or interested in the outcome of whatever was being heard.

A fair number of those seats were occupied, some with people he hadn't met, many with the same ship's captains and merchant captains he'd met in the canteen. Gilpatrick Moore was nowhere to be seen.

Ciarán took a seat at the pleading table.

The clock, an old-fashioned mechanical striker, struck ten.

Ciarán scanned the name placards on the bench. He recognized only two names, Anastasia Blum's, and the guild master's, Isobel Roche. That would be one for, and one against, as Isobel Roche was sister to Merchant Roche from *Golden Parachute*. There wasn't a Truxton, Kavanagh, or nic Cartaí representative on the panel, for fear that the big three would get their way in any argument and the small operators lose out every time. If he were a real person Merchant Leprous would have a better shot at a seat on that panel than Nuala nic Cartaí or Thomas Truxton.

"All rise," someone said, and Ciarán stood, in respect for the institution if not for its instruments, and when Isobel Roche sat, he did.

There was only the one oath in the Federation so there was no swearing in or preliminaries. The guild master introduced the board members and gave their particulars, Annie representing the Merchant Academy and the rest of them small traders, each and every one based out of Unity Station and, until recently, generating the bulk of their income from trade with Ambidex Station.

"That's grand," Ciarán muttered, and it sounded like he'd shouted the words.

"Your microphone is on," the guild master said. "There's a button."

"Thank you," Ciarán said, before muting the device.

Once the introductions were done the guild master gave a little talk about the importance of character in a merchant, and of judgement, and that not all who were accepted as apprentices made merchant, and there was no shame in that. If it turned out Ciarán wasn't accepted for elevation to merchant he might yet try again later, should his apprentice license be renewed. Did Ciarán understand all that?

He said he did, and then said it again, with the microphone turned on. "Before we get into all that," Ciarán said, "There's another matter I'd like to present to the board. The vessel *Thinker's Dame*—"

The guild master cut him off. "We are here to discuss you, Merchant Apprentice."

"We can do that." Ciarán placed the necklace of pendant spires on the pleading table. "The Stationmaster asked—"

"Cut his mic," the guild master said.

Once Ciarán fell silent she spoke.

"I am in charge of this inquiry. I will set the agenda. You are here to answer questions and offer clarifications. Is that clear?"

There was a commotion behind him, people entering, and when he turned to look his heart stopped. Thomas Truxton himself, with the mong hu Thorn, had entered the compartment. So had Fionnuala nic Cartaí and the mong hu Fist.

And Lorelei Ellis.

"Excuse me," Ciarán said, though he doubted anyone heard him, with the mic shut off. He stood and made his way to the rear of the gallery, pausing to allow Thorn to mark his right hand, and Fist to mark his left, as he shoved toward the far rear corner of the gallery, where Lorelei was taking a seat beside Nuala nic Cartaí.

"Merchant Captain," Ciarán said to the head of the nic Cartaí clan, "Pardon me but I need a word with the Ellis of Oileán Chléire."

The guild master started bellowing something, but Ciarán wasn't listening. He'd thought about this long and hard, nearly every night lately, and it couldn't wait.

Lorelei looked magnificent. She'd blossomed, as his brother had said, but it was more than that. She still looked like Laura Ellis, the girl he'd fallen in love with as a boy. But now she looked like she loved Laura Ellis, too. Gone were the shadows of self-doubt, and the anger at being different, and a girl apart. She was entirely herself and not hiding it anymore.

"Laura. What are you doing here?"

"I'm assistant to Nuala nic Cartaí. I'm helping her with the books and she's showing me how to run a mercantile organization. Nice to see you, too, Ciarán."

"Ta. I need to tell you something and ask you something."

"Can't it wait?"

"I swore to myself I'd do this the instant I laid eyes on you."

"Do what?"

"What I'm doing. Come up here and I'll whisper it to you."

She stood and he pulled her a little bit away from nic Cartaí. He'd rehearsed this, a long statement; but when he looked in her eyes, he decided he didn't need to tell her anything she didn't already know.

He asked her, not because he wondered, but because he wondered if she knew. "Are you Folk?"

She looked confused for an instant, then thoughtful, the most Laura of expressions. "I think I must be."

"Me too." Ciarán kissed her and took a step back.

She didn't look any different.

He didn't feel any different.

So he kissed her again. And that time *it took*. When they parted she looked as dazed as he felt.

"I need to go back and finish ruining my career. We'll talk later."

"We'll do more than that," Lorelei said. "Hurry up and take your beating."

Ciarán laughed. "I will. If they kill me, you can avenge me."

Lorelei smiled. "I'd like that."

She would like it too, being naturally fierce, like the wolf pups that sloped around after her at home, watching her night and day, and trying to learn something new.

The guild master was boiling over by the time Ciarán took

his seat at the pleading table. He tapped the microphone. "Is this on?"

It was.

"Good. We'll talk about the *Thinker's Dame* later." He waved his hand in his best imitation of Hector Poole. "Carry on."

Ciarán only half listened as the raging torrent of words washed over him. He wondered what it was about people in high seats that made them revert to the infantile. There wasn't anything anyone could say to him or about him that could harm him, unless it was said by someone he loved and respected. There were only one of those people on the panel and she remained silent.

Apparently the file he'd provided delivered quite a lot of ammunition. That seemed to be the purpose of such files. That practice of distillation and documentation was entirely an importation from the League, and a poor substitute for a good seanscéal, which might not be literally true, but possessed the essence of truth no mere collection of facts could ever rival.

He was expected to answer every now and then, *I will, I did, I won't deny it*, which seemed to make the guild master angrier than if he'd argued with her.

Eventually she ran out of steam. "You're not putting up any defense."

"Defense against what? I did all those things you've listed. I blew out the Ambidex Ring. I made common cause with cannibals. I murdered Merchant Aengus Roche. I lived for years, at the Academy, with a now-admitted slaver. If I was willing to do all those things at the time, at great personal risk, why would I want to apologize for them now?"

Ciarán leaned forward in his seat. "Apparently I misunderstood the entire purpose of this examination. I thought you wanted to meet with me, to talk with me, to *converse* with me, not about the past, but about the future. Would I do a good and conscientious job? Would I put the needs of the crew and the ship above my own? Would I not just recite the Oath, but live it?

"No man can know the future, and I might prove a liar, but that is our skill, isn't it? Winnowing lie from truth, the spoken desire from the unspoken need, the *nice-to-have* from the *can't-live-without*. I thought, as Merchants, you'd want to look me in the eye, and size me up, and judge me for yourself. I had no idea you'd already made your mind up based upon hearsay."

The guild master shouted. "Based on facts!"

"Those aren't facts. They're not even another man's opinion. They're the consensus result of some unknown number of anonymous people opining about events they didn't witness, as reported by people who either didn't care to explain themselves or, like yourself, have an axe to grind."

He glanced at Annie. "The only person who knows the slightest thing about me hasn't spoken a word. That is as it should be. We are Freemen, and we *do not wake the dead.*

"If you were to get on your knees and beg me to take a merchant's license, I would not do it now. I'd be afraid the stink of decay would rub off on me. I cannot believe that I have worked my entire life, have sacrificed and suffered, left my home and my family, signed on with strangers. Risked life and limb.

"I have no one to blame but myself. I believed the lie. And I'm not alone. If my captain were here now. If my crew were here. They would weep at the mockery you make of what we aspire to. You may live as great lords in your shiny station, and pass judgment upon me from your paper throne.

"But be quick about it, because I have places to go, and work to do. Now—"

"I have decided to change my vote," Anastasia Blum said. "This Ciarán mac Diarmuid is not the man I knew." She refused to meet his gaze. "He never was."

The voting took very little time. Seven voices, seven decisions.

"On the question of a Merchant's license for Merchant Apprentice Ciarán mac Diarmuid the licensing board has decided." Guild Master Isobel Roche locked gazes with Ciarán. "On this matter we are one. Denied."

"Denied at this time," Anastasia Blum said.

"Quite so," the guild master said. "Shall we vote on the question of Merchant Apprentice mac Diarmuid retaining his apprentice license?"

Someone shouted from the gallery. "That's not right!"

"Keep out of it," someone else said.

And they did keep out of it. It was the Freeman way. To step over or around. To remain silent. To glance away.

If Aoife had been here, she would have spoken up for him, alone, if she had to. His crew would have spoken up for him.

He wondered if that had been the plan all along, to separate, not him from her, but her from him so that none of his stink would adhere to her, and so that she would not expose herself to censure on his behalf. He glanced behind him, at Nuala nic Cartaí, who sat silently watching him, like a mong hu studying wounded prey.

"On the question of an apprentice license for Merchant Apprentice Ciarán mac Diarmuid the licensing board has decided." Guild Master Isobel Roche locked gazes with Ciarán. "On this matter we are one. Revoked."

Ciarán stood.

The guild master shouted. "Sit down!" A vein in her forehead bulged. "You have not been dismissed!"

"Careful," Anastasia Blum said. "I warned you. He is not the man I knew. He is something far more dangerous.

"What appears to be a pen in his pocket is a blowgun. The hand he hides in his pocket holds a dart, one tipped in deadly poison. If he wished it, you would be dead within a breath, and he vaulting to land beside you, relieving your corpse of that overseer's rod before your body touched the deck. If the rod proved real, and not a wooden facsimile, he could slaughter the rest of us with a sweep of his arm. If it proved wood, he could beat us to death at his leisure. Not a single hand that could stop him would be raised to stop him."

"I don't believe you," the guild master said.

Annie snorted. "What difference does that make? *Look at him.*" She leaned forward in her seat and shouted toward the gallery. "Mr. Moore, how many mong hu are there in this compartment?"

Moore shouted back. "There are four!"

"I counted two," the guild master said.

"Aithníonn ciaróg ciaróg eile," Moore shouted. *One beetle knows another.* "There are four."

"Ciarán," Annie said.

"Merchant?" He hadn't thought about what he'd done but she'd spoken the truth. He did have a death dart between his fingers, and he had considered using it. There was something wrong with the guild master. Something more than enmity toward him. Not evil, not yet, but the seed of evil. She seemed to have forgotten that she served the guild, and not the other way around.

"You wanted to discuss the *Thinker's Dame*?" Annie said.

Ciarán nodded. "The stationmaster said... The *Trinity Station* stationmaster I mean to say, he said that they've identified four of these pendant spires." He held up the chain of earrings. "He asked if I would bring them and leave them with the Guild to see if someone else could identify the other two, or so the Guild might look into if they couldn't." He stepped out from behind the pleading station and moved toward the high bench.

The guild master rocketed her chair backward, away from him.

Ciarán placed the necklace of earrings on the high bench. "That's a burden off me. And the rest of this as well. I can't say I'm happy, but I didn't expect I would be." He glanced from face to face. "I'll be going now, unless there are further objections."

"There is one more matter," Annie said. "Merchant Captain Ruairí Kavanagh informed me that, prior to today, you had no idea how the merchant examination worked."

"That's true. And after seeing it I think it could use some improvements."

"I take it you are also unaware of how merchant captains are selected."

"That's also true. Though I don't see how that matters to me, unless it involves mortal combat with struck-off merchant apprentices."

"That will be all. Guild Master?"

"This inquiry is concluded." The guild master stood, and departed the compartment through a hatch behind her.

The other board members, including Annie, followed her out.

Every Freeman ship's captain and merchant captain in known space seemed to crowd the gallery, all but his own captain. She'd be furious with him when she found out, furious that he didn't at least try to sell his side of the story. He'd failed her, he'd failed the ship, he'd failed the crew.

He'd failed everyone but himself.

At least his dad would be glad to see him. And when his father looked him in the eye he wouldn't find a stranger staring back, but the boy he'd raised turned man. He only wished his mother could be there to greet him. In a way she would be, if Lorelei was there. She'd been a comfort to his mother in her last days, and he was certain his mother would be happy that he had kissed the girl and vowed, in his heart at least, to stand beside her for all the days of his life.

How he would break the news to the ship and crew remained his single greatest worry.

There was a ball-up by the compartment exit, some leaving, some entering. It seemed to take forever but it couldn't be doing so. It just felt that way, with every eye latched on him, and searching his face for some scrap of emotion.

When he'd nearly made it to the hatch the mong hu Fist blocked his way. He turned to skirt around the big cat. The mong hu Thorn blocked his way.

"Come on lads," Ciarán said. "I've had enough drama for one day."

"It sounds like you've had enough for a lifetime." Merchant Captain Ruairí Kavanagh had somehow worked his way through the crowd to stand at Ciarán's elbow.

"Don't believe everything you hear."

"Give it a moment," Kavanagh said. "The crowd will lose interest and soon move on. I *don't* believe everything I hear, you know."

"That's wise."

"I think so. For example, suppose I heard that my sister had become involved with a penniless, dirtball-born merchant apprentice. Suppose I heard that he, like every other man she'd ever grown serious about, wasn't interested in her as a person, but in her inheritance. Or, suppose I heard that he only wanted to use her, and would discard her when he'd had his pleasure. Suppose I heard all that."

"You're Maura Kavanagh's brother."

"I am. She's estranged from the family. That doesn't mean we remain ignorant of her... progress through the world. It doesn't mean that all of us have stopped loving her. Have stopped worrying about her."

"I'm glad to hear it."

"That does not surprise me. For if I had heard any of that I would be inclined to believe it. Certainly more inclined to believe those stories than what Maura told me when I confronted her. Do you know what she said?"

"Ciarán and I are just friends."

"Precisely."

"Maura doesn't have friends."

"She doesn't have *male* friends. She either drives them away or they turn into lovers, for a time, or... appliances of convenience. For when she craves the illusion of intimacy."

"Or they become enemies, who gossip about her."

"Or those. My sister is a difficult person. Difficult to truly know. Difficult to care about. Even more difficult to love, as a brother loves a sister."

"You think she lied to you."

"I know she did. I saw it in her eyes. Fortunately, our mother saw the lie as well. Do you know what she said to me, after Maura had gone?"

"I don't."

"I believe you have a rival."

"For Maura's affection."

"For Maura's *sibling* affection. I'm the only one in the family who can stand her. And she is absolutely wearing me out." Kavanagh held out his hand. "Welcome to our exhausting family, brother."

After they shook hands, Kavanagh removed a handkerchief from his pocket and carefully scrubbed his fingers. "You might find this an interesting fact to share with your own family when you see them next. Do you know what percentage of merchants are ultimately promoted to merchant captain?"

"I'd heard less than ten percent."

"Approximately two percent. Of that two percent do you know how many have been elevated by Guild Master Isobel Roche?"

"I have no idea."

"None." Kavanagh pocketed his handkerchief and patted Ciarán on the shoulder. "It's a trick question."

"I don't understand."

"If the ring does not fit it can be resized," Kavanagh said. "But the coat is one-size-fits none. Attempting to shrink to fit is futile. The best one can do is to be oneself, and hope to grow into it."

Ciarán glanced at his right hand. His fingers were stained black. Stained black with augustinite.

"If Thorn and Fist won't let you out of the compartment don't force the issue. Once everyone else is gone the doors will be locked. At this time tomorrow they'll unlock the doors and either send for a tailor or the undertaker."

"That's how merchant captains are selected? By being locked in a compartment with a mong hu?"

"That is how they are *tested*. They are *nominated* by ship's captains, and *affirmed* by the mong hu. What happens during the test depends upon the candidate. And upon the mong hu."

"That's it?"

"It's a harder test than you can imagine."

"Hard the first time, you mean." And he didn't need to imagine. That was how he and Wisp had met.

"There's only the one time, Ciarán. You don't get a do-over. Any time you want out all you have to do is ask. But if you do ask you won't make merchant captain."

Ciarán's stomach growled. "I haven't had any breakfast. You all kept me talking and—"

"Imagine that." Kavanagh grinned and turned toward the hatch. "Thorn and Fist haven't had any breakfast either."

55

Ciarán met Laura well above the tree line and they hiked the rest of the day to the summit.

He knew she was Laura in that moment because she wore her pensive Laura face and walked along in silence. She remained quite lovely, in her own fierce way, almost regal the way she held herself, the way her gaze swept the horizon. A pair of full-grown wolves trailed her at a healthy distance, uncomfortably close it seemed to Ciarán, but Laura didn't notice, or noticing, didn't seem to care.

It was yet daylight when they reached the Source and would remain so for some hours longer. Ciarán pitched his half tent beside the little crater lake in a flat spot above the rocky strand. The day was clear and cold, the scent of turf-smoke strong while he made a little campfire and brewed them each hot caife.

A bright tiger big as a girl seemed to materialize from a boulder only to disappear again.

"She's not very good at that," Laura said.

A tail thump, followed by a staccato clicking of adamantine claws against rough stone.

Laura's brow wrinkled. "Eat... just ice?"

"Bite me," Ciarán said. "Wisp's self-name is Lady Justice."

"Self-name."

"How she refers to herself. I've explained this already. Click-talk doesn't use pronouns. It's too omnidirectional, and most often used from concealment."

"Lady Justice isn't doing too well at the concealment."

"There's not a lot of cover up here. And the light's very bright."

"Not to mention she doesn't want me to forget she's there."

"Is it going to be a problem? Us having a cat in the family?"

"You don't seem too enamored of my wolves."

"I will admit. I'd like them better if they were on another planet."

She sat down beside him and took the cup from his hands. "And what about me? Did you like me better when I was on another planet?"

"About the same," Ciarán said. "When I thought of you."

"That's a little more truthiness than I wanted."

"You were Macer's betrothed. It was something your mothers wanted. I couldn't fight that."

"You couldn't fight that for me."

"I love you both. You and Macer. I couldn't come between you."

"And what about yourself?"

"If you were happy. If Macer was happy. I was happy."

"Happy with nothing for yourself. With no one."

"I had someone."

"Did you?"

"I thought I did. Though I haven't seen her in a while."

"Maybe I know her. What's her name?"

Laura flinched when Ciarán slapped his hands together. He clicked the clicker he had palmed.

"D-N-T-T." She smiled a half smile. "*The Entity*."

"Have you seen her around?"

Lorelei's smile seemed to light her face. "Tell me again. When did you think of us?"

"I thought of you every night, when you whispered my name on the wind of the world."

"And on those nights I didn't?"

"I imagined Laura had."

Lorelei searched his face. "We aren't... separate people."

"I know. She seems much better, though. She very nearly smiled."

"She smiled. Laura *chose* this. She *asked* that we might be *made whole*. It is only in your memory that she lives apart."

"Only there?"

"We are all of one piece, she and I. Though I think her owed one final dance, alone with her champion."

"I'm no one's champion."

"You nearly beat a man to death when he dared to speak ill of her. You held her hand when the voice in her head tormented her. You made her feel pretty. You made her work to prove she was cleverer than you. When you left her unrequited—"

"I didn't want to hurt her."

"So you punished us both."

"I—"

"Stop." Lorelei punched his sleeve. "We forgive you."

Ciarán smiled. "I brought something for you."

"I can sense it. In your backpack. It grows agitated."

"Sxipestro," Ciarán said.

One of *Quite Possibly Alien*'s spiders clambered from his bug-out kit.

"Oh. Just what I wanted. A large mechanical spider."

"It's also a luminaire. And a weapon."

Lorelei extended a finger toward it. "It's far more than that."

One spidery limb extended. Made contact.

Lorelei sighed. "Fascinating."

"I think it's part of your father. Or your mother."

"It is. And it isn't."

Ciarán stood and walked along the shoreline of the lake. He paused at the lake's outlet, where the waters of the Source tumbled downslope from the headwaters of the stream they called the Willow Bride's Tears.

Somewhere beneath that lake lay the remains of Manus Manusson's experiment, the Between Two Worlds project. Far from being abandoned, the project soldiered on, pumping nanomachines into the lake, and from there into the stream that supplied the bulk of all the water on the island. He didn't know what the microscopic machines did, or how they did it, but he knew they were not enough alone to effect the changes desired.

In addition to being an accidental crash site, Oileán Chléire had proved an ideal place for an isolated biosphere to develop and thrive. Manusson's goal was to create a life form, any life form, capable of integrating biological and synthetic intelligences. The work was far from over but the foundation seemed firmly set. Perhaps not the perfect union Manusson envisioned, not yet, but a step in the right direction. Understanding. Empathy. Perhaps even love. Given enough time anything seemed possible.

Lorelei walked along the shoreline toward him. He met her halfway.

"Well?" Ciarán said.

"It's too... dense for me to fully unpack. I'll need to introduce it to House."

House, one of the wolves howled, and the other, *House*. Seconds later the mountain echoed with the howls of wolves. *House. House.*

Ciarán scratched his eyebrow. "Are they summoning this House?"

The wolves howled again. *House. House.*

"She's nothing supernatural," Lorelei said. "The *Willow Bride*'s computational core. A synthetic intelligence. Presently installed in Ellis H... my home."

"So not an expert system or a genie in a bottle."

"Hardly. She practically raised Macer and me."

"Then what is down there? Under the lake?"

"A starship."

"But the *Willow Bride* was destroyed. The mag bottle—"

"Not the *Willow Bride*. Another starship. A gift for the Knight Commander. Completed, but uninitialized."

"How?"

"Your mother was a *delivery* pilot. Did she not tell you?"

"She did."

"Did you not think to ask her what she was charged with delivering?"

"I assumed it was the *Willow Bride*."

"She delivered the vessel to the *Willow Bride* a week before the disaster. It's down there. Waiting."

"Have you been down there?"

She looked Ciarán in the eye. "I was born down there."

"Huh." He didn't fully understand. And it didn't really matter. Ciarán glanced at the horizon.The sun had nearly set. "It's time."

"You don't have to do this."

"I know it." Ciarán removed his merchant captain's greatcoat and neatly folded it. He began to peel out of his utilities. The air was cold enough he could see his breath.

"Criminy," she said. "It looks like someone's been at you with a power sander."

Ciarán glanced at his arms. "Have you had a close look at a mong hu's tongue? Being licked is like being petted with a rasp."

"They licked you. While you were in the Guild Hall."

"When they weren't fighting over me. It seems my utilities had the scent of Wisp all over them. You know what it's like when two males battle over one female."

"I don't know what that's like."

"I think it was arranged, putting me in that compartment with the two of them. They spent so much time eyeballing and circling each other that they left me alone most of the time."

"And when they didn't?"

"They were affectionate but respectful."

Ciarán peeled down to his socks and boots. He took those off as well, before hoisting a small boulder and hobbling over to the water's edge. He glanced at Lorelei and glanced away.

"What are you doing?"

"Respecting your privacy."

"If I wanted privacy I'd become a hermit. It's a poor merchant who doesn't inspect the merchandise."

"Is it?"

"So Nuala nic Cartaí tells me." Lorelei hoisted a two-handed stone and padded over beside him.

"It's freezing out here," Ciarán said.

"I'm making allowances for that. Can you press that stone above your head? I'll spot you."

"Very funny. I can barely stand upright holding it. Now what?"

"Now we step off and plummet for a long while."

"And then what?"

She dropped her stone, barely missing his bare toes, and dove in, treading water. "Eejit. What do you think we do?"

She splashed icy water in his face.

He took two hopping steps forward and then he was in the frigid water, and falling, her fingers wrapped about his bicep as the weight of the stone in his hands bore them ever downward, until his feet touched bottom, and he released his burden, and she entwined her fingers with his, and kissed him, and clutched him to her breast. He clung to her, and she to him, weightless for a moment, suspended in the shivering darkness utterly devoid of light.

Devoid of stars.

He kissed her, and laughed, air bubbling from his lips, and from hers.

He truly was an eejit. Freed of the stone, there was only one thing he *could* do.

He kissed her again, and held her close.

As united, they began to rise.

ABOUT THE AUTHOR

Patrick O'Sullivan is a writer living and working in the United States and Ireland. Patrick's fantasy and science fiction works have won awards in the Writers of the Future Contest as well as the James Patrick Baen Memorial Writing Contest sponsored by Baen Books and the National Space Society.

patrickosullivan.com

Made in the USA
Monee, IL
05 November 2022

17142659R00163